FALCONER'S WOOD

Before the dusk has formed, an owl swoops across the façade of Falconsgarth, its pale form a clear warning of peril, a warning which Romaine knows better than to ignore. Is not her father dead, and her mother? Who is to be the next victim of the ancient curse which hangs over the Faulkners and is somehow connected with The Wood? Romaine's instincts war with her common sense as she learns of the general resentment against her family and of their long-standing feud with old Connan McIver. To complicate matters, she finds herself attracted to Tom Jamieson, who hates the very name of Faulkner, and her grandmother, in defiance of the curse, orders that The Wood be felled. It seems that nothing will stop the malevolence of Ricard Falconer, who was hanged three hundred years before—as a witch.

MARY MACKIE

FALCONER'S WOOD

ROBERT HALE : LONDON

© Mary Mackie 1979

First published in Great Britain 1979

ISBN 0 7091 7444 6

Robert Hale Limited
Clerkenwell House
Clerkenwell Green
London, EC1R 0HT

Printed in Great Britain by Bristol Typesetting Co. Ltd.
Barton Manor, St. Philips, Bristol
and bound by Redwood Burn Ltd, Esher

ONE

My legs began to ache as I climbed the hill, reminding me that recently they had become unused to such exercise. Up ahead of me The Wood beckoned like a beacon, a tall crown on the knoll, and behind me the valley was spread, verdant and peaceful despite the dampness of the November day. How could my father ever have left it? I wondered as I paused to get my breath.

Not far below me the woods spread prickly branches with only a few withered leaves still hanging precariously, waiting for the next breath of wind to send them tumbling to join their fellows. The gnarled chimneys of Falconsgarth lifted among the trees and beyond them the village clustered, old grey houses set on rambling lanes around the focal point where the main road crossed the river by a low brick bridge. From that height I could see the surrounding fields, some of them ploughed, the combed land waiting for the frost to break down the clods, and some left to pasture for the amiable cows which browsed there while distilling the milk which would soon be thick Devon cream. Higher still, on the slopes of Exmoor, sheep like grey spots of cloud drifted across the rough land.

I breathed the fresh, cold air deeply, thinking that I could have found no better place to recuperate. This was where my roots were, though until a few days ago I had never seen the valley or the ancient house which had been the home of my ancestors for generations past.

Turning to look up at the wood which waited for me, I felt

a pulse of excitement stir my blood, for it was this above everything that I had wanted to see: the place called simply The Wood, whose fortunes were said to be linked with those of my family. How often my father had told me the story, when I was a child and he came to kiss me goodnight

"Yes, Romaine, The Wood is haunted, so they say, by demons and witches. On Walpurgis night a phantom light burns there and anyone who sees it must go at once to the church and pray by the altar until dawn, when all the evil things will depart. And they say that if ever The Wood falls, the Faulkners will disappear from the valley."

Lying safe in my bed, I used to squirm with delicious horror and ask, "But The Wood won't fall, will it? Ever?"

And my father would answer solemnly, "As far as I know, not a single tree has ever been touched. Now go to sleep, you young imp."

The memory brought a sad smile to my lips as I pressed on up the slope, aware of a growing pain in my side. Perhaps it was too soon to have ventured so far, but I had had to come. The Wood tantalised me from my bedroom window, brooding over the house as it did, though I had not realised the climb would be quite so taxing.

The trees seemed to be mainly oak, wide-spread branches giving shelter to a dense mass of undergrowth. It was protected by an ancient fence, broken in places, its uprights buried to the knees in grass where a few late buttercups still braved the chill air. I began to circle the fence, my boots kicking rain-drops from the grass, my eyes searching the depths of the wood, where a mist seemed to hang among the stark branches, creating an aura of coldness that reached out and made me curl closer into my sheepskin jacket.

Only a quarter of the way round, I stopped, staring with a curious shiver of foreboding at an oak which had been neatly split down the middle. One half of it lay within the copse, strangled by creepers, but the other half stood forlorn, dead branches raised in an act of supplication. ' If The

Wood falls, the Faulkners will perish,' the legend repeated in my head.

It was stupid to be superstitious, but all the same I felt suddenly cold as I remembered the terrible dream I had had the night before the accident. The premonition then had come true, for my mother was dead and I had barely recovered from my injuries.

My thoughts were interrupted by the appearance of an old black dog, turning grey round the muzzle, which ambled from the far side of the wood and stopped on seeing me, woofing softly. It was a large animal, part Labrador, paws and tail dripping wet, and as I wondered where it had come from a man strolled up behind it. His slight limp was accommodated by a knobby walking stick, but his height and breadth made him an impressive figure. Streaked grey hair was displayed by the thrown-back hood of a brown parka, while a beard of matching grey brushed the open neck of his shirt. Framed by that hair, his face was wreathed into brown wrinkles.

"Widdershins, is it?" he said in the soft drawled accent of Devon. "Tempting Providence, are you?" Seeing that I did not understand, he gave me a twinkling smile and explained, "Walking counter-clockwise is unlucky. Witches and fairies dance widdershins, when the moon's full."

"Then I'd better go back," I replied half-seriously. "It wouldn't do to tempt fate—not here."

A brown hand lifted to stroke his beard thoughtfully. "You know about The Wood? What are you—French?"

"Half French." Laughing a little, I added ruefully, "I thought my English was perfect until I came here. I gather I have an accent."

"I wasn't complaining," he assured me.

"It was my father who told me about the legend," I said. "He also said not a tree had been touched, but . . ." I gestured at the split oak standing like a crippled giant.

"Aye," he said darkly. "She defied the curse, or tried to."

"She?" I queried.

His eyes snapped back to my face. They were blue, I noticed, very bright and youthful in his gnarled face. But he didn't answer my question.

" Your father's a Winterford man, then?"

" He was. Actually, he was a Faulkner, from Falconsgarth. I'm staying there at present."

He stared at me and for a moment I fancied there was anger in his look before he moved a pace nearer and peered narrowly at me, saying in a strange, quiet voice, " William's lass?"

" Yes." My voice was too bright because I was suddenly nervous. There was something odd about this old man, something that jarred on me. " Did you know him?"

" I knew him," he replied, and sent a glance down at the old house whose ivied walls and upper windows were visible now among the woods below. " Aye, I knew him, rest his soul. I warned her, but she chose to ignore me. Six years and two months ago, wasn't it?" He lifted his walking stick and pointed it at a gash in the bark of the dead tree, a gash which had weathered grey over the years." Six years and two months ago, they came to fell this wood. That was how far they'd got when a bolt of lightning struck. One of the men was killed. And your father died, too."

A part of me was breathless with horror, but the other part —the sensible English half—was arguing that it could be mere coincidence, an accident enlarged upon by superstitious minds. There could not be a connection between men taking an axe to this tree and my father inexplicably drowning in a friend's bathing pool. But I looked up at the jagged branches of the tree and I felt again the intense chill of the place, lifting the tiny hairs on the back of my neck.

" But surely . . ." I argued, as much with myself as with him, " you don't believe that the death of this tree caused . . . It's only a legend."

" A legend. Aye. Then how do you explain it? Your father believed in it, you know. It was because of The Wood that he finally left. That shook her, so she delayed her plans, but six years and two months ago she started on it again."

I began to suspect that 'she' was my grandmother, and I was spellbound by the old man's doom-laden voice. "I'm not sure I follow you," I said uncertainly. "My father said he left Falconsgarth of his own choice. That was before I was born, before he even met my mother."

"You look cold, lass," was his reply. "My wife'll have the kettle on. Do you fancy a cup of tea?"

The change of subject disconcerted me. It seemed odd to hear that he had a wife. I had been about to decide that he was a hermit, set to guard The Wood.

"You live near here?" I asked.

"Down there." Again the knotted stick pointed, to an arm of the woods which ran along the foot of the hill. There was a narrow side road climbing up from the valley and where the woods ended a small cottage stood, a thread of smoke whispering from its chimney.

It was perhaps two hundred metres around the hill from the cottage to Falconsgarth, not far, and I had left grandmother busy with phone calls on behalf of one of her committees. Somehow I was in no hurry to return to the big house, but a rest would be welcome for the pain in my side had become like a sharp, hot knife.

"I'd like that," I said, "if you're sure your wife won't mind."

"She'll be glad of the company. It's been a long time since we had a Faulkner under our roof. Here, Maidie! Come on, girl."

The obedient dog came waddling to heel down the hill, and my companion strode out as if it were level ground, only slowing when he realised I was having difficulty in keeping up with him.

"In pain, are you?" he enquired with concern.

"A little," I admitted. "I only came out of hospital two days ago. That's why grandmother brought me here. She didn't want me to go home until I'm fit again. It's silly, but you don't realise how weak you are until you try to do normal things."

Gravely, he offered me the support of his arm, which I

accepted with a smile of gratitude. It had been foolish of me to make that climb alone.

The cottage was surrounded by a low wall in which a gate was set, leading to a path which bisected a vegetable patch and lawn. On the washing line four shirts hung limply in the damp air, begging for a breeze.

"Ruth!" the old man called, opening the back door and ushering me inside, where the warm air was full of the scent of freshly-baked bread and cakes. Wire cooling racks were piled with baking; the furniture was old but well cared-for; and there was a pleasant homely atmosphere aided by an untidy knitting basket and a pile of car magazines thrust on top of the Welsh dresser.

In answer to another call of her name, a woman emerged from a dark hallway, smoothing back her fairish hair. "I'm sorry, I was making beds," she smiled, and held out a hand as her husband introduced me. "So you're Miss Faulkner. Goodness, aren't you pretty? Make yourself at home and I'll put the kettle on."

"I hope I'm not putting you out," I said and, seeing her disconcerted look, explained that I had an accent because my mother had been French.

"Of course. I'd forgotten. You speak very good English— oh!" She blushed prettily, laughing at her own confusion. "I expect you speak both."

"Bi-lingual," the old man said with a gentle smile.

"That's right," she agreed, turning back to me with a wink. "Oh, Con knows all the big words. Makes me wonder why he ever married a pudding-head like me."

The open affection which surged between them made me feel warm and contented. This was a happy home, I was sure, though Ruth was considerably younger than her bulky husband. Her movements were quick and deft although she was plump, and her eyes sparkled in her rosy face.

"Miss Faulkner's just come out of hospital," the old man told his wife as he shrugged off his parka to reveal a darned sweater. "That's why she's here—to convalesce."

She shot me a sympathetic look, tutting under her breath. " I'm sorry to hear that. Been poorly, have you?"

" It was a road accident," I explained, remembering that grandmother had told me to be careful how much I said. The last thing she wanted was a horde of reporters descending on Falconsgarth. " My mother was driving. She . . . wasn't as lucky as I was."

" Oh, dear! That's terrible. I am so sorry. What a terrible thing! And were you in hospital long?"

"Almost three months."

" Now, Ruth," her husband chided, taking a chair opposite me at the table, " let the poor girl get her breath. The village may be agog for news of Miss Faulkner, but . . . "

" What do you take me for?" she exclaimed indignantly. " Are you calling me a gossip, Connan McIver?"

He slanted a grin at me through his beard. " You're a female, aren't you?"

" And *that* to you," she retorted, slapping him on the head with a knitted tea-cosy which she then fitted onto the tea-pot. " That's men for you, Miss Faulkner."

I found myself laughing with them. " Please . . . call me Romaine. My father used to talk about you, Mr. McIver. I didn't realise who you were. You worked for my grandfather, didn't you? As a shepherd?"

The twinkle died from his blue eyes, replaced by a shadow. " Man and boy. Over thirty years. Many's the time your father walked the hills with me when he was a boy. He loved this place. It's a pity he had to leave."

" He always said that he left to find a life of his own," I said, puzzled, " because uncle Walter would take over Falconsgarth."

" Aye." His look added ' if you say so '. Clearly he didn't want to contradict the version my father had given me.

The old dog had padded up beside me and laid his head in my lap. I stroked the whiskered ear absent-mindedly, watching Ruth McIver pour tea into thick willow-pattern cups.

"There was something else, wasn't there?" I said in a low voice. "I always did wonder, but he would never go into details."

"Your father was loyal," Connan McIver told me, adding three spoonsful of sugar to his cup. "It's not my place to bring out the skeletons. Let the past go, Romaine."

The past. I glanced out of the window and there on the hill The Wood was wreathed in mist, dark and ominous, and something shuddered across my soul. Whatever the English half of me might say, the superstitious Burgundian half, with its roots deep in the folk-lore of the vine-clad hills, was tossing uneasily, stirring up the Romany blood which came from my great-grandmother Dupris and which had given me the dark hair and eyes I possessed. Was it only weakness and heightened imagination that made me suddenly restless?

"Do have a cake," Ruth interrupted my thoughts, thrusting a laden plate in front of me. "Eat and grow strong. And don't worry about that old wood. 'Tis all nonsense."

"You don't believe that," her husband said quietly.

She glanced sharply from my face to his. "Con! You didn't go and tell her . . ."

"Why not? She has a right to know. What happened, happened. You can't deny that. Six years and two months ago. Almost to the day. Your mother saw it, Ruth."

"My mother was a very old lady who couldn't hardly see to the end of the garden, let alone right up that hill! Who knows what she saw?"

"Are you saying Ben Freeman lied—about his own brother? Ben was there when it happened. A bolt of lightning from a clear blue sky . . ."

"Con!" Her voice was taut with worry. "There's no call to go frightening Miss Faulkner. There was thunder about that day. They were foolish to be so near those trees. And as for Mr. William, why . . . why that was chance, nothing more."

"Aye," he replied, and supped his tea.

The cakes were melt-in-the mouth delicious and I ate three, trying not to think about the significance of the dead tree. It *was* irrational to believe that some age-old curse could reach across hundreds of miles and cause my father to drown, though that accident had never been fully explained to my satisfaction. It had been a hot day, a few friends gathering round the poolside, and my father had always been an excellent swimmer. No one had understood how suddenly he came to be on the bottom, unnoticed for a time, when he hadn't been drinking heavily or doing anything which might have caused him to drown.

But if the curse had been going to work, why hadn't it struck nearer at hand? Grandmother was a Faulkner, and so were uncle Walter and aunt Lydia, not to mention my cousin Peter. If the dead tree had had to be avenged, why had the power not worked on one of them?

The confusion in my mind stopped as the back door was flung open and a young man stepped in, bending his dark head to avoid the lintel.

"Why, Tom!" Ruth exclaimed in pleasure. "You're early."

"Let off for good behaviour," he said with a grin, one arm around her shoulders as he dropped a kiss on her forehead. "Hello, Con, I . . . Oh, I'm sorry. I didn't realise we had visitors."

"Only one," Ruth corrected, beaming. "This is Miss Faulkner, from Falconsgarth. This is my son Tom, Miss Faulkner."

"Romaine," I said, leaving my seat and holding out my hand before I noticed the frozen look which had wiped the smile from his face. He hesitated just long enough for it to be noticeable, then shook my hand perfunctorily and turned away to hang his leather jacket on a peg behind the door.

The atmosphere seemed to have become unfriendly and had I not had a second cup of tea waiting on the table I would have made excuses and left. As it was, I sat down again stirring my tea reflexively.

"Romaine has just come out of hospital," Connan McIver said.

"Oh, really," Tom replied in a disinterested voice. "Is the tea still hot, Mum? I'm dying for a cup."

"Then sit down and talk to Miss Faulkner. You're not shy, are you?" Despite the teasing words her tone was pleading, begging him to be polite.

'My son', she had said, though he seemed to be around thirty and I would have guessed her age as no more than mid-forties. But whatever the explanation his hostility towards me was all too evident and I swiftly drank my tea before glancing at my watch. It was just after four o'clock.

"I didn't realise it was so late," I said. "Grandmother will be wondering where I am. Thank you very much for the tea, and the cakes."

"You're very welcome to call any time," Ruth replied with a smile. "But you can't walk home alone. It's getting dark. Tom will go with you."

I saw from the stiffening of his frame that Tom would do nothing of the kind, so I protested that it was not far. I would be perfectly safe walking round by the road.

"I wouldn't feel right," Ruth said, and her jaw was set. "Thomas—you'll take Miss Faulkner home, won't you?"

"He hasn't had his tea," I objected. "Really, I . . ."

"He can have a fresh one when he comes back," she said firmly.

Tom planted his hands on the table and rose heavily from his chair. "That's right, mother. I can. I'll be delighted to walk Miss Faulkner home." It was said with so much emphasis that it sounded sarcastic, as he meant it to be, but to save further argument I kept silent. Clearly his mother wished him to be courteous.

Thanking them again, I stepped through the door which Tom held open with his foot as he pulled on his jacket. The mist was thickening and the day rapidly waning as we walked in silence round the cottage to the front gate which led onto the lane. Once on the road he set such a pace that I could not keep up with him. His legs were longer than mine and he was obviously fit. When he realised I had dropped behind he stopped and turned to wait for me, hands deep in the pockets of his worn jeans.

" I can manage perfectly well alone," I said. " I'm sorry your mother made such a thing about it."

He looked at me from under dark brows, lips curling slightly with contempt. " She wouldn't have done if you hadn't been a Faulkner."

" If I hadn't been a Faulkner," I replied steadily, " you wouldn't have objected to coming. Would you? Not that it matters. I can go alone."

As I started past him, a vehicle came roaring up the road, headlights blazing in the dusk. We stepped onto the verge to let it pass, but it screeched to a halt just beyond us and backed until it was level. It was the Falconsgarth Land-Rover and driving it was my cousin Peter.

He flung the nearside door open and leaned across to say angrily, " Where have you been, Romaine? I've been looking everywhere. Grandmother's worrying herself silly. Oh, save the explanations. Get in."

" That appears to solve your problem," I remarked to my unwilling escort, who shrugged and bent to look at Peter.

" Good evening, Mr. Faulkner," he said with meaningful politeness.

Peter ignored him. Hardly waiting for me to get in, he leaned an arm across me and slammed the door, sending the Land-Rover into a swift three-point turn that made Tom leap out of the way. It also wrenched my side and brought back the pain across my ribs.

" Is that how English gentlemen behave these days?" I gasped.

Peter gave me a black scowl and then sighed. " I'm sorry, but when it started to get dark we were concerned about you. And then to find you with that . . . "

" You mean Tom McIver?"

" God!" His laugh was harsh. " Don't let any of them

hear you say that. He's known as Tom Jamieson. McIver may be his father, or his grandfather. Nobody's exactly sure. But since his mother was unmarried when she had him he uses her maiden name."

"How could Mr. McIver be his grandfather?" I asked, puzzled.

"Easily. He lodged with old Mrs. Jamieson for years but he only married Ruth after the old girl snuffed it. So anything's possible."

"That's a horrible thing to say," I objected.

"Well, life's horrible. Human nature's horrible. Romaine, what are we arguing about that lot for? Are you all right? You look a bit pale."

He was turning the Land-Rover in between the tall, wrought-iron gates in the wall which guarded Falconsgarth itself. The lights cut a swathe through the darkness beneath the trees as we swung round the long drive and saw the frontage of the big, angular house. It was all outcrops and buttresses outside, as it was full of passageways and unexpected nooks and crannies inside, and the stout grey walls were covered in the long creeping shoots of ivy.

We found grandmother in the red sitting-room, taking tea with my aunt Lydia. A log fire gave out the aromatic scent of pine and two lamps shed arcs of light across the crimson carpet and up the heavily-patterned wallpaper.

"So there you are!" grandmother said softly, turning at our entrance. "Come and sit down, my dear. You must be frozen. Where on earth have you been all this time?"

She patted the chair beside her with a pale, slender hand and I obediently slid into the seat.

"I found her with Tom Jamieson," Peter said.

"With whom?" aunt Lydia exclaimed, her long face etched with disapproval. "Really, Romaine . . ."

"He was bringing me home, because it was getting dark," I said. "It was a courtesy."

Grandmother sent a repressive glance at my aunt. "As long as you're safe, my dear. Have a cup of tea."

Since she had already poured it, it would have been churlish to refuse. The cup was bone-china, as fragile as my grandmother herself. That afternoon she wore a pink trouser suit with a blouse whose fichu was scarcely whiter than her halo of hair. Many another woman nearing seventy would have looked ridiculous in such an outfit, but grandmother had the figure of a girl and her skin was still clear.

"And how did you happen to be with Tom Jamieson?" my aunt asked tartly as Peter threw himself down on the settee and accepted a cup of tea.

"I went up to The Wood," I replied. "I met Mr. McIver and he asked me back to his cottage for tea. His wife . . ."

"You didn't *go*?" aunt Lydia exclaimed in horror. "Mother, haven't you warned Romaine about that family? Why, McIver's raving mad, and as for that immoral 'wife' of his . . ."

"I had no idea Romaine would run up against Mr. McIver so soon," grandmother said. "Besides, Lydia, taking tea with them is hardly a major sin. On the surface they must seem a perfectly normal family."

"Oh, they do," Peter put in, "but Romaine really ought to check with us before she goes visiting. She knows absolutely nothing about the people here. I'm not trying to put a curb on you, Romaine, but really you ought to be more careful, for your own sake."

"Careful of what?" I asked, but nobody bothered to answer.

"I suppose he was trying to fill your head full of his nonsense," my aunt said, looking down her large nose at me. "You mustn't believe a word he says. The man is not entirely sane. And he has a grudge against this family which has been going on for years. Whatever he told you, I suggest you ignore it."

"Romaine isn't a child," grandmother reminded her. "She has a sensible head on her shoulders. Though you do look a little tired, my dear. It was foolish of you to go so far on your first outing."

Shamed by the gently reproving tone of her voice, I said,
" Yes. I'm sorry."

As I sipped my tea, which I didn't really want after two
cups of Ruth's strong brew, I considered this family whom I
had recently acquired. Grandmother Faulkner, despite her
delicate watercolour appearance, was still the head of the clan.
Everyone else deferred to her, even aunt Lydia, who was
a rough-hewn woman, solidly built and with little femininity.
She wore severe clothes and not a trace of make-up to enliven
her sallow complexion, which was not helped by the man-
nish way she had her greying hair cut. My father had always
said she was ' all high principles and tight corsets ' and apparently time had not changed her much.

My cousin Peter was more difficult to read, for I had not
seen much of him in the two days I had been at Falconsgarth.
Physically he was an attractive man some five years my senior,
with neat brown hair and hazel eyes fringed by luxuriant
lashes. He managed the estate for grandmother and to me he
had been pleasant and charming—until that day, when I
suppose his temper was caused by anxiety for my safety.
They all seemed to feel responsible for me.

As for my uncle Walter, my father's older brother, what I
had seen of him had not impressed me. He seemed to be in
awe of both his wife and his mother and spent his days
closeted away in a study. At mealtimes he said very little but
kept his eyes on his plate, having a hang-dog air. It was one
of the small puzzles I had discovered at Falconsgarth—why
did not uncle Walter manage the estate, rather than his son?
I had expected to find him a slightly older version of my
father, but he was different in every way.

Listening to the conversation, which was about some local
matter of which I had no knowledge, I wondered if I should
raise the question of the legend and find out the truth about
the dead tree. But something prevented me, for I knew what
they would say—that it was nonsense, coincidence. And they
would probably be right.

It was later, after dinner, that grandmother herself raised

the subject of The Wood. As we left the dining room she drew me aside, waiting until the others had departed before she closed the door and gave me a kindly smile.

"Romaine, just between ourselves, I'd prefer it if you did not get too closely acquainted with the McIvers. I'm not blaming you at all, don't think that. It's my own fault entirely for not warning you. But there could be danger, for yourself. Connan McIver is an enemy of this family. It may suit him to be nice to you at the moment, but his motives may not be all they seem. What exactly, did he tell you?"

"You mean about The Wood?" I asked. "I already knew the legend. That's why I wanted to see it for myself."

"You saw the dead tree?"

"Yes."

A hand tipped with pearl-pink nail varnish rested lightly on my arm and there was sympathy in grandmother's grey eyes. "He told you that I caused your father's death, didn't he? I ordered the trees felled, so my son died. Romaine, that is pure superstition. You can't believe that. It's true that a man was killed when the lightning struck. It is also true that a few days later we had that terrible telegram which told us your father had drowned. But to connect the two because of some legend that is only folk-lore and hearsay . . . which apparently has no sound reasoning behind it . . . You surely don't believe that? You're a modern young woman. These are not the Dark Ages. It is a myth. Only a myth."

"Why, yes," I said, and I sounded surprised that she could doubt it. "Yes, of course it is."

"I'm very glad to hear you say that," she approved. "Those are valuable trees, mature oaks, most of them, and at present a little extra cash will be of use to me. In a few days' time some men are coming to cut down that wood, all of it. And then we shall be rid of that silly legend once and for all."

TWO

I did not sleep well that night and consequently when I woke it was late, past nine o'clock, though I had been told not to worry about sleeping in. I needed as much rest as I could get.

Having showered in the adjoining bathroom, I pulled on a pair of jeans and a thick sweater, because Peter had said something about showing me round the estate—unless he had grown tired of waiting for me. I drew back the curtains and gazed through the leaded windows at the sombre woods behind the house. Above them The Wood loomed, standing sentinel over Falconsgarth. Was that it? Did the trees act as guardian to the Faulkners? Despite my assurances to grandmother, I hated the idea of The Wood's being destroyed. If nothing else it was a beautiful thing which must have stood on that hill for hundreds of years. And if the legend were true . . .

Great-grandmother Dupris, I thought ruefully, you and your gypsy blood have a lot to answer for. The death of a tree cannot cause the death of a human being. Yet deep inside me there remained the uneasiness which had been with me ever since grandmother told me she intended to have The Wood felled.

A movement on the hillside caught my eye and to my surprise I saw uncle Walter out there on the slope. A moment later another man came into sight, with an old black dog at his heels. The two were deep in conversation, Connan McIver waving his stick towards The Wood, obviously disturbed. It seemed very odd, for uncle Walter talked little with his family. What could he be discussing with Connan McIver?—The 'enemy', as grandmother had called him, though it occurred to me belatedly that she had not explained *why* he was our enemy.

Shrugging to myself, I put this further little mystery to the back of my mind and went down to find Peter waiting to have breakfast with me before taking me for a tour of the estate.

I was shown the sheep and cattle which belonged to Falconsgarth; the pastureland and the arable fields; the farm-workers' cottages and the Home Farm where the under-manager lived. The estate covered a wide area on the edge of Exmoor and included a narrow, tree-filled valley with a stream, which was beautiful but unfortunately produced no profits, though Peter said he was looking into the possibility of raising game-birds there.

"Couldn't you just leave it?" I asked as the vehicle toiled up the hill out of the valley. "It would be wonderful for picnics."

"Oh, it is," my cousin said drily. "For other people, though. They park themselves there every summer when the beaches are full. But that doesn't help us—unless you're suggesting we should pay someone to sit and take an entrance fee."

"No, of course not. It just seems a pity to spoil it."

Peter slanted a grin at me, hazel eyes alight with amusement. "You obviously don't have a business mind, Romaine. But don't change. Cold-bloodedness wouldn't suit such a beautiful girl."

"And what about The Wood?" I added, ignoring the flattery. "Aren't there other trees that could be cut?"

"Not like those. Anyway, grandmother is tired of having that stupid legend hovering over her. Personally I think that wood is an eyesore. I mean, it looks so peculiar standing alone on the hill."

For me, part of The Wood's charm was its 'peculiarity' its failure to comply with the rules when all the other hills around it were bare. But I didn't argue. It was, after all, none of my business, because my father had chosen to leave. When grandmother died the estate would go to uncle Walter and after him to Peter. I had no claim, nor did I want one.

"Well, that's the end of the tour," Peter said. "I've got some business to do before we go back for lunch. It won't take long. I have to see a neighbouring farmer about a bull. And we might see a friend of yours."

"A friend of mine?" I queried, laughing. "I don't know anyone."

"You know Tom Jamieson."

"Oh. I hardly 'know him', Peter. We met, for about five minutes. He didn't say a civil word to me."

"He wouldn't. He's got a chip on his shoulder a mile wide. Comes of having such a questionable ancestry. Anyway, he works for old Halliday, so unless we're lucky we may run into him."

We were coming down into a wide valley which, unlike the Winterford vale, had scarcely a tree in it. The hills on either side were rocky, bare shoulders protruding from the tough grass, and there were no arable fields beside the road, only grazing for cattle and sheep. When we were still half a mile away from Halliday's farm, Peter pointed out the low white building to me. It was set back against the hill-side, surrounded by outbuildings, and a rough, puddled drive led up to the farm-yard.

"Wait here, will you?" Peter asked as he parked the car. "I'll see if Mr. Halliday is well enough to see me. He's crippled, and sometimes he doesn't feel up to much."

I watched him stride to the brown-painted door in the white wall, which opened and admitted him; then, feeling the need to stretch my legs, I climbed from the vehicle and leaned against the door, sheltering from the chill wind as I watched the speckled chickens scratching between the cobbles. Nearby, a cat stopped washing itself beside a water-butt and came padding languidly towards me, to sniff at my shoes in an enquiring fashion. It was a beautiful animal, tawny and slim, muscles rippling beneath its fur, and as it lifted its head to look at me with bright green eyes I bent to stroke it.

"I wouldn't," a voice said, and as I glanced up the cat lashed out with its claws and drew blood from the back of my hand, making me gasp and straighten in a hurry, putting the hand to my mouth.

Tom Jamieson had come from the barn and was standing regarding me with a cold smile. "Don't you know better than to play with a farm cat? That one's practically wild, doesn't let anyone handle it—even a Faulkner. Is it bad?"

I looked at the scratches. Two were bleeding, but only a little. "No, it isn't. No doubt you'd have been more pleased if he'd taken my hand off."

"As long as you don't expect me to play Galahad and bind the wounds with my hanky," he replied. "What's he come for? About the bull?"

"He?" I repeated, bridling. "Your family has a strange habit of never referring to my family by name, except as Faulkners. Do you mean Peter?"

"Who else would I have meant?" he returned.

Presenting my back to him, I said wearily, "Yes, he's come about the bull."

"Ah."

I turned round to face him, seeing him watching the house expectantly. The breeze flapped his dark hair across his forehead, but he looked formidable, broad and rock-solid, long jean-clad legs planted apart in wellington boots, the leather jacket open though it was a cold day.

"Tom . . ." I said placatingly. "May I call you Tom? I wish you would tell me what you have against me. And don't say it's because I'm a Faulkner because that doesn't explain anything. Besides, my name is Romaine."

He moved his head so that he was facing me squarely, and his eyes flicked over me insolently. When they returned to my face I saw grim amusement in their depths, and before I knew what he was about to do he had stepped forward, grabbed me by the shoulders and kissed me, hard. Face burning, I pushed him away, scrubbing at my lips with the back of my hand, my heart thumping unsteadily with alarm.

"I thought you were asking for that," he informed me calmly. "Don't flirt with me unless you mean it, Miss Faulkner."

"Flirt?" I got out.

"Isn't that what you were doing?"

"No, it certainly is not! I was trying to make friends, but I don't think I want to be friendly with you. I could sue you for assault!"

Grey eyes glinted as he stared at me under lowered brows. "Indeed you could, though I would say I was provoked. You should be careful of talking too much. That accent is very sexy. Can I help it if I got the wrong impression?"

Furious, I marched away from him to lean on the stout fence which edged the drive. The back of my hand stung and was turning mottled blue with cold, so I thrust my hands into my pockets and hunched my shoulders against the breeze blowing along the valley.

Although I was aware that Tom Jamieson had followed me and was braced against the fence a few feet away, I ignored him, wishing Peter would come.

"That's the bull, in the far field," my unwelcome companion informed me. "He's a fine animal."

"I really wouldn't know," I said loftily. "Especially from this distance. What are you, anyway? The cowman?"

"No." His tone revealed that he was having trouble keeping his temper. "I'm the manager."

Tossing my hair, I turned so that the breeze was in my face, cold against my skin, and I leaned both elbows on the fence behind, saying to the hills, "Then go away and manage. I don't need your company."

There was silence. He let out a heavy sigh and strode away, stopped, and after a moment's indecision came back to the fence, where he bent to snap a stem of weed from the long grass by the fence.

"Miss Faulkner . . ."

I turned my head, careful to keep my expression blank. He was holding the weed out to me, his arm along the top of the fence. Among the small leaves there were tiny blue flowers.

"Speedwell," he said. "Pretty, isn't it?"

Clearly the weed was an attempt at a peace offering, but my nerves still burned from the imprint of his lips and the strong hands that had clamped on my shoulders, so I shook back my hair and looked away along the valley.

"I suppose a Faulkner expects two dozen red roses," he said bitterly. "I'm trying to ... What do you want me to do —go down on my knees?"

"You can lie on the ground and kiss my feet!" I stormed, furious with him. "It still wouldn't make up for what you did."

"What—one kiss?" His lips curled and he glanced down at his spread hands. "Of course. I dared to lay my dirty plebeian hands on a Faulkner. They should be chopped off at the wrists for being so insolent."

"Oh, go away!" I said, tired of him. "Take your inferiority complex elsewhere, will you?"

He took one huge stride towards me and his hand shot out to fasten on my chin, making me look at him.

"You've got it wrong," he said in an undertone lined with fury. "It's you and your family who have delusions of grandeur. Who do you think you are? Just because your grandfather was knighted for being good at killing people ... "

Incensed, I slapped his arm away. "I know who I am. Who are *you*?"

The words, thoughtless as they were, seemed to pierce him. There was sharp pain in his eyes and only then did I remember his clouded parentage. As he began to turn away I flung out a hand to stop him.

"Tom! I didn't mean it that way. Please ... "

At that moment we heard Peter's voice saying goodbye to the farmer. Tom shrugged away from my touch as my cousin appeared round the Land-Rover, smiling in satisfaction.

"Sorry to have been so long, Romaine. The business is completed, I'm glad to say. I'll send the truck in a few days, and our cheque will be in the post."

"For how much?" Tom wanted to know.

Peter named a figure which seemed ridiculously small to me until I realised he was talking in pounds and I was thinking in francs. But Tom Jamieson seemed to be of the same opinion for he was staring incredulously at my cousin.

"How much?"

"You heard what I said," Peter returned. "Did you expect us to pay over the odds, just because it's for Falconsgarth?"

"That's way below the market price, and you know it," Tom said angrily. "You know Mr. Halliday's in a hole, don't you? He's old and he's sick . . . "

Bridling, Peter demanded, "Are you accusing me of taking advantage? The price is hardly your concern, Jamieson. Your employer and I have shaken hands on it. Shall we go, Romaine?" He took my hand and tucked it under his arm, frowning at me. "Goodness, girl, you're cold. Why didn't you wait in the car? Good morning to you, Jamieson."

"Good morning, *Mr.* Faulkner," Tom replied, eyes bitter and his mouth twisted with a disgust which was directed equally at both of us as we turned away towards the waiting vehicle.

"He's got a nerve!" Peter muttered as he started the motor with an angry flick of the wrist. "And what was going on between you? I could have cut the atmosphere with a knife."

"He dislikes us all," I countered. "To him I'm just another target because my name is Faulkner. Why is that, Peter? What have we ever done to him?"

"I told you—he's got a chip on his shoulder, and he's infected by Connan McIver. Like father, like son. Basically it's pure envy. It's as petty as that."

I didn't believe him. Somehow I was sure that Tom Jamieson was not the type of man to be so bitter for such trivial reasons. So what was the answer? Why did he hate the very name of Faulkner?

The episode of the bull took on an even more unpleasant aspect that afternoon, when there came a phone call from Mr. Halliday to say that he had decided he could not part with the animal at the price he had tentatively agreed with Peter. After consideration, he wanted more money, or he would offer the bull elsewhere.

Peter was fuming as he burst into the red sitting-room to tell grandmother of this development. "After consideration!" he spat. "He means after being got at by that damn Jamieson. I had a feeling he'd throw a spanner in the works."

"Calm down, Peter," grandmother said, laying aside her book. "Did you have anything in writing?"

"No, of course I didn't. It was a gentleman's agreement."

"But Henry Halliday is not a gentleman," she observed. "And neither is Tom Jamieson. Offer him half of the extra. If he won't take it, withdraw the offer. There are other bulls."

"Yes, but not at . . . " He stopped himself, with a glance at me. "Oh, very well, grandmother. You're the boss."

As he left the room, she turned to me with a little laugh. "The boss, indeed! But there you have an example of the enmity of Tom Jamieson and Connan McIver. Both of them will do anything in their power to cross us. It's quite tiresome."

No, I thought, that isn't entirely true, because Peter had almost said they could not buy another bull 'at that price', which meant it was low. Perhaps Tom Jamieson had had right on his side. It left an unpleasant question-mark hanging over my cousin's ethics.

"Have you any interest in flower arranging?" grandmother said suddenly.

I looked up from my magazine, startled. "Flowers? No, I'm afraid I know nothing about it. Why?"

"Because tomorrow your aunt and I will be arranging the flowers in church, for the commemoration service on Sunday. We do it every year on Remembrance Sunday. Your grandfather died on November the eleventh, you see. It will be twenty-six years tomorrow since he passed away." It was said in a reverential tone, with a suspicion of tears in her eyes.

It must have been shortly after grandfather's death, I calculated, that my father had left Falconsgarth for ever. Was there a connection? It was in my mind to ask grandmother for explanations, but the words were not said, for the same reason I didn't question her opinion of Connan McIver, because it might have been tactless of me to blunder into areas whose pitfalls I could not guess.

" Why did I leave home?" my father used to say when I asked. " Oh, you know how it is. The estate only needed one manager and your uncle Walter was doing that. So I went off to seek my fortune and met your mother. And then you came along, my little one." He would smile and touch my nose with a tender finger. " My home is here now, with you."

Another time I remember asking him about Falconsgarth as it would be then, who lived there, and he had said, " No one who matters to me. Not any more." Small wonder that I had been astonished when grandmother Faulkner arrived at the hospital to see me for the first time. I had thought her long dead, because every time I asked about Falconsgarth my father would answer vaguely and add, " When I was a boy . . . "

Yes, I reflected. Now that I came to think about it, all the detailed stories he had ever told me about Falconsgarth had happened when he was a boy. He had never told me anything about his later life, nor about his mother, though his father had often figured in the tales.

In the library there was a life-size portrait of my grandfather, General Sir Gerald Faulkner. Grandmother had shown it to me and I was suitably impressed by the handsome soldier in his scarlet dress uniform with rows of gleaming medals. He had a sandy moustache and he was trying to look stern, but the artist had caught a quirk of the lips and a gleam in the eye, so that it always looked as if the General were about to burst into laughter. I felt that I would have liked him enormously.

It had been unfair of Tom Jamieson to sneer at the knighthood given ' for being good at killing people '. In the past, so my father had said, the Faulkners had been barons and lords, with lands of which Falconsgarth was only a small part. The titles had drifted away from our branch of the family until grandfather was knighted, but we were still an old family, documented in many history books, going back several centuries in recorded history. The family name, it was said, had once been Falconer, so perhaps we originated from an ancestor who had kept the king's falcons and received honours for his work—that was what we liked to think. Nobody knew for sure.

However, I was to discover a little more about the family history, for to my surprise I was invited by uncle Walter, after dinner that night, to accompany him to his study and look at the albums.

" A good idea," grandmother approved. " But don't keep her too long, Walter. She needs her rest."

" Yes, mother." His vague blue eyes turned back to me and he smoothed back his hair in a nervous gesture that was becoming familiar to me.

I followed him through the narrow passages to the library, where a door in the far wall was concealed by bookcases which swung open as my uncle pulled a knob. He ushered me inside the study, which was bewilderingly untidy, books and papers strewn everywhere, pens and pencils thrown on the desk, a waste-paper basket overflowing. The air was thick with the smell of stale smoke, making me cough.

" I'll open a window," my uncle said, and did so, letting the cold night air slide into the room under heavy curtains. " They don't like me to smoke in the other rooms, so I'm afraid I rather tend to over-indulge in here. I hadn't thought. Is it too bad?"

His eyes were anxious and I wished he wouldn't constantly apologise for his very existence.

" It's fine. They do badger you a bit, don't they?"

" With reason," he said mysteriously. " Sit down, Romaine.
Here, let me move those books."

The pile of magazines, dumped on the floor, slithered
into a heap, but he didn't seem to notice. He took off his jacket
and exchanged it for a baggy brown cardigan, then asked my
permission to light a cigarette.

" Well," he said, blinking at me from behind the desk and
a wreath of smoke. " Well, so here you are. William's girl.
Never thought I'd see you at Falconsgarth, never in my life.
You're like your mother. She was a beauty, too."

" You knew her?" I asked, surprised.

" Oh, yes. That is, no. We met the once, in Paris. Just
after they were married. William asked us over but mother
wouldn't go and Lydia was pregnant. The child died. It was
a girl. I'd have liked a daughter." He sent me a quick, nervous
smile. " Still, you didn't come here to listen to me ramble,
did you?"

" It would be nice to talk," I said. " I never seem to see
you, except at meals, and then grandmother and aunt Lydia
hog the conversation. Do you come in here to escape from
them?"

It was meant as a joke, but my uncle sighed and shook his
grey head. " Where else can I go? It's better to keep a low
profile. And I'm contented enough, pottering. It makes me
feel useful."

My mind was full of questions which I was on the verge
of asking when he suddenly got up and reached to the top
of a book-case to take down three leather-bound volumes
which he placed with loving care on the desk.

" I've spent months doing these," he said, his hands
caressing the tooled leather.

" Photo albums?" I asked.

" That's right. We had a whole pile of our own snaps and
then I came across a box-full in the attic. Took me ages getting them properly sorted and marked, and I'm still not up
to date." He glanced across at me and for the first time

since I had known him he looked animated, enthusiastic. " We must have a shot of you, now you're here. I've got a film needs finishing. We'll do that tomorrow. Now . . . this is the first. Careful with it! "

The leaves of the book were dark brown, thick card, and on them the photographs had been neatly set and labelled in a copper-plate hand in white ink.

" Did you write these? " I asked.

Uncle Walter looked pleased as he nodded and came to crouch beside me, pointing out pictures of particular interest. There were sepia prints, somewhat blurred, of ladies in bustles, carrying parasols, and gentlemen in top hats and frock coats. ' Henry Faulkner, circa 1902 ' was seated proudly in a horseless carriage, beaming beneath a handle-bar moustache.

Before I had looked at half of them, my uncle took the book away and gave me the next, saying that he mustn't keep me from my rest. He seemed afraid that grandmother might come in and reprimand him.

In the second book there was a record of the wedding of my grandparents, he in uniform and she with a shingle hair-cut and flapper dress. She looked absurdly young.

" She was just eighteen," uncle Walter told me. " He was thirty-five. She says he fell in love with her when she was ten and waited for her to grow up, but I don't know how true that is. Look, that's me in my sailor suit, and here's your father in his pram with *my* grandmother. She was a dear old soul, and . . . Now wait, you didn't see your great-great-uncle William, did you? You mustn't miss him."

He reached for the first album, flipping through its pages until he found the one he wanted, then laid the book on my lap. The photograph was of a grossly fat man wearing one of those bathing suits with sleeves and knee-length drawers. He had a long beard almost to his waist and on his head was a solar topee.

" *Merde*! " I laughed.

" He's a character, isn't he? " uncle Walter agreed with a

quick grin. "Lived to be a hundred and four, so I'm told."

"Where did you get all this information?" I queried, impressed. "You can't remember all these people."

"No, but I've had help. There's an old lady in the village, over ninety now, who was a kitchen maid and then cook at Falconsgarth. And . . ." as he hesitated, he glanced towards the door with a queer, crafty look, "And there are one or two others," he concluded swiftly.

Fascinated, I flicked past a few more pages of the older photographs, slipping a finger in as a picture different from the rest caught my eye. I laid the page open, staring at the dark sepia tones which seemed to depict a carving of a leering face with horns and a long tongue flicking out to one side. Beside it, uncle Walter had penned an artistic question-mark.

"Oh, that," he said, seeing my interest, "I don't know why I put that in, except that it's quite old."

I peered closer, holding the book so that the light fell directly onto it. "Is that a tongue, or a flame?"

"It's the Devil," my uncle said in an undertone. "Can you read the words underneath?"

Squinting, I saw there were two words, with perhaps a ' b ' in the middle of the first one. The face grinned obscenely at me and suddenly a feeling of unease crept over me. There was evil in that stone face with the baleful eyes. Shivering, I snapped the book shut.

Uncle Walter looked up into my face, his eyes narrowed. "It gets me that way, too. Funny. It's only a photo. I keep meaning to ask Dick . . . someone I know who's interested in photography."

"I thought it was just me," I said. "Mother was very superstitious, and my French great-grandmother is supposed to have had second sight—she was a Romany. Maybe I've inherited some of that, or," I smiled ruefully at him, "maybe it's just my vivid imagination."

"Is that where your name comes from? Romaine—Romany? I'd no idea. You are very dark, of course, but I thought that was the French blood. Your father was fair." He ran a hand through his own grey hair, leaving it more tousled than ever. " So was I, once."

His thoughts seemed to be troubling him, so I asked to see the final album, which was only half full. There were pictures of uncle Walter's wedding to aunt Lydia, then Peter as a baby and a growing boy, and, surprisingly, a colour shot of my parents in a garden.

" I took that when I was in Paris that time," my uncle told me. " They were very happy, weren't they? They'd only known each other three months when they got married."

" They always said it was love at first sight," I replied, smiling at the memory. " They were very close to each other, even though mother was often away on location. After father died, she was in a terrible state. She didn't care about anything. I think that's why she started making those terrible sex films. They made her rich, but they didn't make her happy."

" They say she was on drugs," my uncle said unhappily.

" Yes, I know they do. It may have been true. She was in a peculiar frame of mind when she came over here for that publicity tour. For one thing, she insisted that I should come with her, when she'd ignored me for ages. She said something about wanting to make up for lost time. I have wondered . . ." I hesitated, because I had never told anyone else what I suspected. " Perhaps she knew she didn't have much time. She believed in premonitions. She was . . . intense, high-strung, those last few days."

Silently, my uncle reached out for a newspaper which was tucked under the book-case, smoothing it out so that I could see the headline: ' Sex Star in Death Crash '. Lower down there was a picture of mother at her most glamorous.

" It says her secretary was with her," uncle Walter said. " We tried to get in touch with you in Paris, and your employers told us you were over here with her. We had trouble finding out the truth."

" Yes, you would. Her agents suppressed the fact that she had a daughter, especially one of my age. I mean, a thirty-

B

five-year-old sex symbol can hardly have a daughter aged twenty-three and remain credible, can she?"

" I wondered about that. They lopped a few years off her age, did they? Not that she looked older than they said. She was still a beautiful woman."

" She worked hard at it." Realising that I sounded bitter, I said no more. It is a terrible thing to admit, but there was little grief in me over mother. She had been like a stranger to me during those last few years and I did not approve of the films she made or the string of lovers she had had to keep up her image. Even though I knew she had done these things because she was heart-broken after losing my father, I could not understand. She had not let me share her grief. Rather she had resented my own feelings of loss, as though I had no right to mourn her husband. Her belated attempts to make things right by dragging me along on her British tour and buying me expensive presents had only emphasised the wide gap between us.

A heavy sense of oppression was on me. Sensing it, my uncle put away the newspaper and we looked through the remaining photographs in the album, though I was no longer really interested. These people had little to do with me. My father had rejected them. What on earth was I doing at Falconsgarth?

" This will be a fascinating record for your grandchildren," I said eventually. " Thank you for showing them to me."

" There's just one more thing I'd like you to see, if I'm not keeping you from your bed." He rose stiffly to his feet and fetched a square box which he gave to me. " One of the family heirlooms. The turnip watch. Real silver."

Opening the box, I took out the heavy watch, marvelling at the craftsmanship of the dappled case which felt cool and smooth beneath my fingers.

" Careful with it," uncle Walter cautioned, watching me anxiously. " The lid opens here, see. Mind."

The watch face was ornate, slender hands against a painted circle with Roman numerals, and inside the lid was inscribed

' John Henry Faulkner, May 19th 1856 '. Seeing it, I knew why I had come to Falconsgarth. Part of my heritage was here and I was curious about the family history. The big watch in my hands was evidence of that.

" It's beautiful," I said, holding the watch lovingly, aware that it must be immensely valuable for it was in fine condition and over a hundred years old. Some silversmith had carefully hammered and tooled the case into a work of art.

" It's always handed down to the oldest son," my uncle said, and I could feel his relief as I returned the watch to its box. " That's become the tradition. It goes to the heir."

So some day the turnip watch would belong to Peter, I thought with a pang of envy as I handed the box back.

" It's beautiful," I said again, and my uncle gave me a quick smile before carefully returning the watch to its place on the shelf.

" I've enjoyed our talk," he told me. " I hope I haven't kept you too long."

" Not at all." I stood up, shivering a little in the draught from the window. " We must talk again. There are a hundred questions I want to ask you, uncle Walter, but to be honest I'm too tired now. I think I'll get to bed."

" Of course. You need your rest. We want you to be fit and well. That's true, you know."

Surprised, I looked at him and discovered a worried look on his face. " I never doubted it."

" Romaine . . ." he said anxiously, grasping my wrist, his eyes no longer vague but alive with concern. " Romaine, be careful."

" I will," I said, and leaned to kiss his cheek, leaving him looking bewildered, one hand touching the place where my lips had rested. " Good night, uncle Walter."

I sought out the other members of the family to wish them goodnight and climbed the stairs to my room feeling depressed and weary, wondering how long it would be before I felt fully well again. The pain in my side had become a nagging ache which never entirely left me, but at night it grew worse and I was glad to lie down.

Worried about The Wood, I drew aside my curtains and looked up at the dark hill, where the trees were outlined against the wind-tossed clouds. I had meant to ask uncle Walter what he thought of the legend, but it could wait. The men would hardly come to fell trees at the week-end.

As I was about to drop the curtains back into place, I froze and stared, my scalp prickling with apprehension. There was a light up by the copse, moving slowly along with a jigging motion, just above the ground. Memories of my father's tales came strongly—'a phantom light burns there on Walpurgis night.' Except that it was not Walpurgis night, the eve of May Day, it was November.

Troubled, I moved away from the window, belatedly wondering at the significance of that strange warning from uncle Walter. 'Romaine, be careful.' What could he have meant?

THREE

I spent another restless night full of strange dreams of foreboding and woke in the darkest hour to hear the wind buffeting through the trees and sweeping the Exmoor hills with an almost-animal yowling. In the blackness that pervaded the room I lay awake, tasting my fear to see what it was made of and finding no comfort in my thoughts.

My instincts were all on edge, warning me of a danger which I sensed but could not name. It had been there ever since I arrived at Falconsgarth, though by day it lay beyond the edge of my consciousness, a vague shadowy feeling which in the darkness of night I could feel like a pulse beneath the rhythm of life. I was afraid, and I didn't know why.

Reaching for the wrap which lay across the foot of the bed, I slipped it round my shoulders and walked through the darkness to the window. There was nothing outside but the night in which I could hear the wind, the trees tossing restlessly. Perhaps it was the wind that had disturbed me, for like a cat I was always irritable and jumpy when the wind blew wildly. At least there was now no light in The Wood.

In the grey morning light, with rain sliding down the window, the sensible English half of me took charge once more. If I was uneasy, it was because Falconsgarth was still strange to me and I was not strong. How my father would have laughed at the old fancies which kept invading my mind, though mother would have said they were warnings. Warnings of what? I was safe here—except that soon they were coming to cut down The Wood.

No, that was ridiculous. Legend and superstition, no more. I repeated the assurance to myself until I almost believed it, then I went down to breakfast.

During the morning I was in the library writing a letter to some friends in Paris, under the benign gaze of my grandfather's portrait, when aunt Lydia strode in.

" The flowers have come," she announced. " Do you want to see them?"

" Flowers?" I said vaguely.

" For the church. It's the commemoration service tomorrow. Mother said she told you. Do you want to see them, or not?"

She stood behind my chair, reading my letter over my shoulder. Irritated, I closed the pad and got to my feet. " Yes, I'd love to."

I suppose she could not help the fact that her face had a constantly disapproving expression, but it did not endear her to me. She was sharp-tongued and critical and I wondered

how on earth my uncle Walter had come to be married to
such a dragon.

The flowers had been put in the morning room, where
grandmother was sorting them into different buckets—waxy
Arum lilies, red and yellow roses, and a few long-stemmed
chrysanthemums with shaggy bronze heads, besides ferns and
leaves for greenery in the arrangements. I made approving
noises, while grandmother described the effect she intended
to produce in church.

"Your grandfather was a patron to the village," she told
me, "and I feel that we, as Faulkners, should make an effort
this one day a year, to remind people of everything Gerald did
for them. Oh, and by the way . . ." She reached behind her for
a long box which lay on the table. "These are for you. From
Peter."

"Peter?" The box was green, labelled on the front
'Hathersage, Florist' and addressed to me at Falconsgarth,
I removed the lid, finding a dozen red roses still dewed
with moisture beneath their cellophane wrap. "They're
lovely! But why should Peter . . ."

"My dear Romaine," grandmother interrupted, laughing.
"Why does any man buy a girl flowers?"

"But he's my cousin," I objected, amazed by the gesture.

"And so? He's a man and you're a very attractive girl.
Take them to the kitchen, my dear. Amy will give you a vase.
You can put them in your room, if you wish."

Aunt Lydia gave me a strained smile but said nothing, so
I couldn't guess what she thought of this extraordinary token
from her son.

I wasn't at all sure what I thought, either. Peter had never
given me any hint that he might like me in any special way
and it could be extremely embarrassing if he was going to
start paying me this sort of attention, for I felt nothing for
him. Nothing at all.

In the vast kitchen, I showed the flowers to Amy and she
found me a vase, saying only, "Pretty, aren't they?" and
then continuing with her work. She was a taciturn woman

who kept the house efficiently and unobtrusively, so I knew nothing about her.

I set the flowers by the window in my room, thinking ruefully that grandmother would probably have made a better job of arranging them. It was entirely possible that she had misconstrued Peter's motives; he was most likely trying to cheer up the invalid. At least, I hoped that was why he had sent the flowers.

Outside, the rain had stopped, though the sky remained leaden. There was still a remnant of last night's wind left and it shook the branches in the woods. Up on the hillside I caught sight of a lone figure in a brown, hooded coat, walking with a slight limp as he leaned on a walking stick. There was no mistaking the massive figure of Connan McIver.

As I watched, he stopped and stared down at the house, so I opened my window and waved, consciously ignoring grandmother's warnings. The McIvers had been kind to me and until I found them otherwise I had no intention of listening to vague hints of scandal. I waved again, knowing he could hardly fail to see me in my scarlet jumper against the darkness of the ivy, but he gave no response and eventually turned away towards his cottage.

Puzzled, and a little hurt, I watched until he was out of sight. Perhaps he had been deep in thought, not really looking at the house. But somehow I was sure he had seen me and had deliberately ignored my distant greeting. After his previous friendliness, such a snub seemed strange—unless Tom had reported my haughty attitude of the previous day.

Peter was late for lunch and we began without him, but within minutes the Land-Rover pulled round in front of the dining-room windows and grandmother excused herself, saying she must have a word with Peter about a business matter.

"Something going on?" uncle Walter asked mildly as grandmother left the room.

"Nothing that concerns you," his wife replied.

He looked as though she had hit him. At once his head drooped and he concentrated on his soup, while I glanced at aunt Lydia wondering why she had to slap him down at every opportunity.

"So you won't be helping with the flowers," she remarked, managing to make of the comment an indictment.

"I'd only make a mess of them," I said. "But I wouldn't mind coming with you. I haven't seen the church yet."

"No point in coming just to stand around. It will be cold. You'd be better off staying indoors. You still look very peaky."

My uncle lifted his head again, to look hopefully at me. "We could get that photograph taken, if you like, while it's fine."

"What photograph?" aunt Lydia demanded.

"I thought it would be nice to have a picture of Romaine to add to the album," my uncle said almost apologetically. "It won't take long, or tire her."

"You and those stupid albums!" his wife scoffed.

His eyes met mine, in them a sad little gleam before he gave his attention to his plate and didn't speak again for the entire meal.

Feeling sorry for him, I said reasonably, "The albums are a wonderful record for future generations, aunt Lydia. If uncle Walter hadn't rescued the pictures when he did, they might have been lost, or it might have been too late to identify them."

"You're obviously another dreamer," she retorted.

The discussion was interrupted by the return of grandmother, with Peter. He apologised for his lateness and sat down next to me with a smile.

"How are you today, Romaine?"

"I'm fine, thank you," I replied. "And thank you for the roses, Peter. I've put them in my room, but I think I'll bring them down so that we can all see them. They're really lovely."

"I'm glad you like them," he said, glancing at grandmother, who smiled benignly on both of us.

Immediately after lunch, Peter went back to the Home Farm, where some problem with the men had arisen. Grandmother and aunt Lydia loaded the flowers into the boot of grandmother's white Granada and with injunctions to me not to overtire myself they drove away through an afternoon that was turning brighter, the sun trying to break through.

When I had seen them go, I went straight to the library and the book-covered door of the study, to stir uncle Walter from his hibernation in order to take the picture that he wanted.

We made our way through the house to the back door, which opened onto a leaf-strewn lawn. The land sloped up from there to the woods some twenty metres away and the watery sun was lying pale across the tree-trunks, warming the air just enough to make it pleasant.

I posed against the trees and he took two shots of me before deciding that he would like to photograph me against the front of the house; so we returned through the passageways and found a sunny spot on the ivy-covered wall for a third picture.

"One left," my uncle commented, looking at the camera. "It's a long time since I had my picture taken. Would you mind . . . ?"

"I'd love to," I said, and changed places with him. "Smile!"

"It's just for the record," he objected.

He looks very serious in that picture. To see it now gives me an odd feeling.

"Is there a chemist in the village?" I asked.

"Not one who develops photos. We'll take it to that friend of mine—I mentioned him last night. Dick Handley. We'll have them back by Monday if I go today."

"What, now? May I come?"

"Do you want to?" he asked, brightening. "Yes, do. It's not far. Dick lives in the old mill down by the river. You'd better put a coat on."

A few minutes later we met in the hall, I in my sheepskin jacket and he wearing a shabby old raincoat and flat cap. I had a feeling that aunt Lydia would have shuddered to see him, but my reaction was a wave of affection which made me tuck my hand beneath his arm as we walked down the drive.

Our way lay along a twisted lane with cottages almost hidden by trees, and eventually we came out onto the High Street, where the few shops were set back behind wide grassy areas. The main road curved across the end of this street, and there we turned right, towards the river, pausing on the low bridge to look at the swirling water below.

The mill lay on the opposite bank, a large structure of red brick behind a rough yard where a shed stood rotting, its tarred planks gaping at the seams to show glimpses of old boxes inside. There was no millwheel, but I could see the place where it had been, above a sluggish pool filled with weeds.

"The river dammed up there, so that the race came through that channel," my uncle told me. "But it hasn't worked for ages, not in my life-time. The old wheel rotted, but Dick reckons he'll build a new one, when he finds the time."

We crossed the uneven yard and climbed the steps to the peeling door, where my uncle knocked loudly. A few moments later the door was opened by a long-haired woman in paint-spattered jeans and a loose sweater.

"Lovely to see you, Walter. I'm afraid Dick's out. Was it Dick you came to see?"

"Just came to leave a film for him, if he's got the time to do it for us. This is my niece Romaine, from Paris."

"Paris, eh?" She grinned as she shook my hand. "Nice to know you. I'm Jill."

The big room was a mess—there is no other way of describing it. Two small children sprawled on the floor, daubing paint onto large pieces of yellow paper. A loom stood in a shadowy corner; there were toys and books, bits of wool, and in another corner a cot contained a sleeping baby.

"Chaos, isn't it?" Jill laughed. "I keep threatening to clear the whole lot out and start again, but it never gets done. Will you have a cup of tea?"

My uncle refused, politely, glancing at his watch and saying we really mustn't be long. I guessed that he was worried in case his wife should return before we did and demand an explanation for his absence. However, he gave Jill the film, slipped a coin each to the two older children, and we left the mill.

" The family don't like my being friendly with Dick and Jill," he explained. " They're . . . unconventional, and they're newcomers. Dick was trained as a solicitor, but he gave it up and now he does odd gardening jobs and some photography, and Jill does weaving. I got to know them five years ago when . . ." He left the sentence incomplete, almost biting it off.

" Do you care what the family think?" I asked.

" No. Except that . . . " Again he stopped himself, leaning on the low parapet of the bridge. " Oh, it's difficult, Romaine. You probably think I'm spineless, but I prefer a quiet life. After what happened . . . I'd rather not make waves. It's best for everyone."

" What did happen? Can you tell me?"

He straightened, sighing, and gave me a wan smile. " Oddly enough, I think I can. You're not like the others. You're like your father. I could have talked to William, if he'd been here. He was always stronger than me. If only he'd been the oldest, then none of this . . . Shall we walk? We might go round by the church and see if they've finished the flowers. We can say we came out for a walk."

" Good idea." I took the arm he offered and we turned towards the village centre. " So what happened five years ago?"

" It was then that everything blew up in my face. I was a fool. I've always been a fool, Romaine—that's why mother had me marry Lydia, to calm me down. That's really the root of it. I should never have married Lydia."

We came into the High Street, walking past the butcher's and the greengrocery to the little wool shop. Very few people were about on that Saturday afternoon, most of them having gone into Ilfracombe, or Barnstaple, or even Exeter for their weekend shopping.

"Are you prepared for a very sordid story?" uncle Walter asked, his mouth awry with self-disgust.

"I don't believe it can be all that sordid," I replied softly. "You aren't that sort of man."

"Aren't I?" His laugh was deeply bitter. "Thank you for that, my dear, but I must disillusion you. As William's daughter you have a right to know the truth. Besides, just once before I die I'd like someone unbiased to hear my side of it. You see, Romaine, I was . . . I was an alcoholic."

Incredulous, I stared at him.

"Oh, yes," he said sadly. "It's true. Why do you think my son is now the estate manager?—Because I made some very stupid and expensive mistakes . . . Because of me, they're still struggling—though don't ever reveal that you know.

"I managed to keep it to myself for a while, but five years ago the auditors found I'd juggled the figures. I was so scared of what would happen that I went on a bender and ended up in hospital. When I eventually came home, things were as you find them now—Peter had taken over my job and it was made clear to me that I must never put another foot wrong, or else! Like Esau, I sold my birthright for a mess of pottage, and now I'm left with nothing."

"Then why do you stay at Falconsgarth?" I asked. "You could go away, take a job, recover some self-respect."

When he looked at me I saw the tears in his eyes. "I'm fifty-one, Romaine, Who would have me? I just count myself lucky to have a roof over my head and food to eat, and solitude to potter about my own interests. I haven't the guts to break out."

Not knowing what to say, I hugged his arm to my side. It wasn't all his fault, I thought. Instead of helping him when he needed it, his family had ground him further into the dust and made sure he stayed there. After five years of such treatment it was no wonder he was without hope.

I was about to ask whether his story had any parallel with
my father's leaving home, but he stopped and pointed to the
church lying at the head of the road behind a row of black
yews. The white car was still parked outside it.

"You go and see how they're getting on," he instructed.
"I'll go home. I need a smoke and I've forgotten my
cigarettes. Go on, my dear. You said you wanted to see the
church."

Saddened, I watched him walk away, a hunched figure in
his shabby raincoat and cap, hardly one of the proud Faulkners
of Falconsgarth. All my sympathies were with him, for I
sensed a kindred spirit in many ways and perhaps, after all,
he did remind me of my father, just a little. They both had
the same kindness.

There was a lych gate set in the wall of yews, its roof protecting the seats set either side of the pathway. The gate
squeaked as I pushed it open and went through to climb the
shallow-stepped pathway beyond, between rows of weathered
tombstones, to the shelf of the hill where the little Norman
church stood solid, its porch open to the air, sheltering a
studded door that was blackened by time.

It was cold in the church, with that usual feeling of peace
and stillness deepened by centuries of reverence. High, narrow
windows let in the pale sunlight and by the altar my grandmother and my aunt were busy over two bronze urns of
flowers. They had already filled a vase by the lectern with a
display of chrysanthemums.

The church was not very large. Hard pews stood each side
of the central aisle where a strip of worn matting was laid,
and behind the back pew a shelf was fixed, holding a box of
postcards and a few pamphlets telling the history of the
church. Since I had some loose change in my pocket, I took
one of each and dropped the coins into the box which stood
ready.

The clatter of the money echoed through the church, causing my grandmother to look round and call, "Hello, Romaine.
We're doing very well, don't you think?"

Since I had no wish to raise my voice in that hushed place, I merely waved and nodded, turning to look at the memorial stones placed in the walls. Near the opening into the bell-tower, where more flowers waited in a plastic bucket, I found a plaque with my grandfather's name carved and picked out in gold. On the same stone, bringing a knot of foolish tears to my throat, had been added, 'And his younger son, William Anthony Faulkner, 1930-1972'. There was space, too, for other names, the marble waiting for more deaths to mark its smooth surface, and I found myself remembering The Wood, standing sentinel for centuries, about to be destroyed. . . .

The letters of the two names seemed to stand out sharply, but the rest of the world had become a blur. All at once I knew the reason for the underlying dread which I felt at Falconsgarth—the legend was true: if The Wood fell, so would the family. And across the picture came another, redolent with unholy laughter, an evil, leering face with horns and a long tongue.

The blood rushed from my head and the daylight appeared to wane; then a hand touched my arm and I jerked round to stare unseeingly . . .

"Why, Romaine!" grandmother's voice said in concern. "My dear, what's wrong? Are you unwell?"

My eyes focused and with an effort I shook away the darkness, but such was my confusion that I answered her in French. "*Ce n'est rien. Je*... I mean, yes, I'm quite well, thank you. I felt ... a little faint. It's passed now."

For a moment she frowned, then understanding came into her face as she glanced at the memorial tablet. "That's it, of course. You didn't know your father's name was here. I'm sorry, my dear. I should have warned you, but after all this time ... You've shivering. My dear, I do wish you would take things more easily. Why don't you sit down and wait for us? Or would you rather go back to Falconsgarth? Amy will make you a nice cup of tea. That's right. It would be the most sensible thing. Put your feet up and relax for a while. Maybe

Peter will be home soon, and Lydia and I won't be much longer."

Still dazed, I wandered to the door and went out. I don't think I even answered her, for the presentiment of danger was still on me strongly, rippling through my nerves.

In the cool sunlight I blinked away the last of the veil of foresight and looked around me at the world of reality. I felt the aura of coldness from the ancient stones behind me, lying across the graveyard. The hills looked faded with autumn; the yews stood dark; the village street curved away, edged with grey stone houses. And I saw The Wood, etched against the pale sky, alone on its knoll. Watching. Waiting.

So great was the feeling of doom that when I saw Ruth McIver bending over a grave some yards away I had an opposite reaction of immense relief and pleasure. Here was someone friendly and smiling, untouched by the evil which I was now sure was hanging over Falconsgarth. I hurried along the path to speak to Ruth, eager for normality.

"Ruth! Good afternoon!"

She was setting white chrysanthemums into a vase on a grave whose stone read 'Annie Jamieson, aged 83. Rest in Peace', but she glanced round with a smile—which died when she saw me.

"Good afternoon, Miss Faulkner," she said distantly, and went on with her task, her headscarf flapping in the breeze, her hands red with the cold.

A feeling of *deja vy quenced* my spirits and I remembered how Connan McIver had also turned away from me. I ventured to the side of the grave, enquiring quietly, "Your mother?"

"Yes."

"They're beautiful flowers, aren't they? From your garden?"

The last bloom positioned, she stood up,, stretching her back as if it were aching, not looking at me. Without another word she hobbled away on legs that were stiffened by crouching.

I opened my mouth to speak again, but the high-pitched screech of the lych gate interrupted me. Glancing across, I saw Tom Jamieson come striding up the path towards his mother, though he hesitated when he saw me and at the same moment Ruth looked over her shoulder.

"Miss Faulkner . . ." Her eyes were unhappy. " I don't mean to be rude, but . . . It's unfair. It's cruel and unfair."

Before I could enquire as to the meaning of this remark, two swift strides had brought Tom to her side. He took her arm, turning her away from me. " Go and get in the car, Mum. I'll tell Miss Faulkner what happened."

" Well, keep your temper," she begged. " No more trouble, Tom, please! "

" There won't be any trouble," he promised. " Go ahead. This won't take long."

We both watched Ruth's retreating back as she made her way down to the gate. She seemed to have aged overnight, I thought.

" Well?" I prompted Tom.

His head snapped round to fix me with granite-like stare. " No, it's not well, Miss Faulkner. It's not well at all. Your family may own this whole damn area, but there are some things not even a Faulkner can do with impunity. It's about time your grandmother found out she's not God Almighty! "

" My grandmother?" I repeated, bewildered by the attack. " Is this about the bull?"

" No, it's not about the bull! Though in case you're interested we've had another offer for it—a fair offer. The bull won't be coming to Falconsworth."

" Peter was trying to cheat you, wasn't he?" I said quietly. " I'm ashamed of him. But it was nothing to do with me, Tom. And I'm sure grandmother didn't understand what he was up to. An old lady like that can't be expected to know the market price of livestock. That's what she employs Peter to see to."

He lifted a sceptical eyebrow. " Oh yes? Well, I'll take

your word for it. I suppose that old lady wouldn't know anything about rat poison, either."

"Rat poison?" I echoed.

"Or something of that kind. Poison, anyway, laid down around The Wood. I had intended to go to Falconsgarth myself, but if I had run up against your cousin I might have lost my temper. You can pass on a message for me. Tell them it worked. Maidie's dead!" He spat the words as though they had a bad taste.

"Maidie?" My mind struggled to understand the implications of what he was saying. "Maidie's *dead*?"

"Do you have to keep parroting everything I say?" he demanded. "Yes, Maidie—Connan's dog, in case you'd forgotten."

"I hadn't forgotten!" My own temper was loosing its rein. With one thing and another my nerves were in shreds; I was cold and the ache in my side was spiteful. "I just don't follow you! Can't you forget for a moment that I'm a Faulkner and talk to me coherently?"

He frowned deeply, grey eyes cold, but when he spoke his voice was calmer. "I'll try. Connan and Maidie have made a habit of walking up by that Wood. They've done it for years, until Maidie thought it was her own territory and went wandering up there nearly every time time she was out. She never did any harm. Well, last night she went missing. I found her, eventually, up by The Wood—dying!"

"I hope you're not suggesting that it was done deliberately," I said hotly. "That's ridiculous! They wouldn't. . . ."

"Wouldn't they?" he interrupted. "Use your head, woman. They hate Con. They'd do anything to hurt him. Why else would they lay poison at The Wood?"

"There could be lots of reasons. I wouldn't know. You're wrong, Tom! Nobody could have planned for Maidie to get poisoned—if there was any poison."

"There was," he assured me, his voice deep with disgust. "You have a lot to learn about your precious family, Miss Faulkner. They're not known as the Devil's breed for nothing.

Your grandmother came to it by marriage, but she's as tainted as the rest of them—worse, if anything."

I realised I was trembling, with cold and with fear. "Do you know what you're saying? You expect me to believe... You're mad!"

"No." He shook his head slowly, almost sorrowfully. "It's you who are naive. But you'll learn. Then we'll see how much of a Faulkner you are. Con says your father was different. Maybe you are, too, especially when the Faulkner strain is mixed with good red gypsy blood."

"How did you know that?" I gasped.

He shrugged. "Con told me."

"And how did _he_ know?"

"He knows lots of things. Goodbye, Miss Faulkner." With one last glance from flint-like eyes, he turned away.

"Tom..." I faltered, and he stopped, looking at me across his shoulder. "Why do they call us ... 'the Devil's breed'? That is what you said, isn't it?"

"It is. Does it bother you?"

"I'd like to know."

Turning up the collar of his leather jacket, he stared for a moment at the squat tower of the church. "It goes way back. Cruelty, injustice, evictions, harsh taxes—you name it, the Faulkners have done it. And there was one of your ancestors who was hanged as a witch. The name has stuck—though I don't suppose the present family are too anxious to let it be known. It's too close to the truth."

"You're horribly prejudiced, you know," I told him. "Do you always believe the worst about the Faulkners?"

"I've learned to do just that," he said, but the steel in his eyes had softened fractionally. "Do you want a lift back?"

I shook my head. "No, thank you. I can walk. I'm sure we shall all be happier that way."

It was as well that I decided to walk back to Falconsgarth, for it gave me time to think over what Tom Jamieson had said and to calm myself. I could feel the two halves of me struggling for supremacy—the dark, mediaeval beliefs in the old gods and the forces of darkness warring with the Protestant thinking which my father had made sure was stamped on my soul. I longed for guidance, for someone to tell me which was right, for the turmoil was pulling me apart.

Glancing back at the church, I saw it with a golden halo of sunlight as the sun dipped behind the tower. It seemed like a blessing, soothing my tortured thoughts. The Wood was merely trees. Summer lighting had killed the unfortunate woodsman. My father had died by accident, as before him other Faulkners had died, untimely or of old age, without so much as a branch in The Wood being disturbed.

But Romaine, whispered the other half of me, it was in the church that the power came to you, warning you.

Pure suggestion! I replied furiously.

But already the Falconsgarth drive was filled with shadows and the tall trees on either side breathed together as I passed. And as I came in sight of the house a pale form swooped across the ivy-clung walls and I stopped, my heart slowing to a murmurous beat that chilled my blood, for the form was an owl, out before the dusk had properly formed. Bird of ill omen, bird of the night: it was a bad sign, a warning sign. I could no longer doubt my instincts.

FOUR

"Romaine!" Peter's voice hailed me from the front door. "Hurry up. Amy's just made some tea. What are you staring at?"

My pulse resumed a more normal rhythm as I crossed the forecourt. "There was an owl."

" So? Haven't you seen an owl before?"

" In broad daylight?"

Peter glanced up at the sky. "Hardly broad. Anyway, it does happen. Maybe something disturbed it." Hazel eyes met mine appraisingly. "You look pale. Are you cold?"

" I always seem to be cold," I said, stepping past him into the warmth of the hall.

The log fire had been lit in the sitting room. I stood by it, rubbing my arms, looking at the lovely roses which Peter had sent for me. They stood now on the tall mahogany table by the wall, surrounded by bronze jugs that gleamed in the light from one of the standard lamps. But my mind was not on the flowers; it was on an old greying dog which two days ago had nuzzled my hand as I stroked its head.

" Aren't you going to pour?" Peter asked, nodding at the coffee table where the silver tray was set.

" No, you can."

" Me?"

His tone of astonishment reached through my thoughts and made me look at him. "What did you say?"

" I said . . . Oh, all right, I suppose I can do it. What are you—Women's Lib. or something?"

" I just didn't hear what you said." Still abstracted, I sat down on the settee, trying to rub some life into my cold ankles. "Peter . . . I saw Mrs. McIver and her son in the churchyard."

The stream of tea stopped as he lifted his head to stare narrowly at me. "You've been told to avoid them, Romaine."

" I know, but it was only polite to say hello. Peter . . . Connan McIver's dog was found poisoned last night."

He continued to pour.

" Up at The Wood," I added.

" Milk?"

" Just a little. Did you hear what I said?"

" I'm waiting for you to get to the point," Peter said levelly, handing me a cup. "Biscuit?"

" No, thank you. You don't seem surprised, or concerned.

An old man lost his faithful dog, on Faulkner property, because there was poison."

Picking up his own cup, he moved from the fireside chair and sat down beside me, stirring in his sugar. "Romaine, that old man had no right to be on Faulkner property. I'm sorry if his dog got some of the poison, but he should have taken better care of it."

"You knew there was poison?"

"Of course I did! There are rats in that wood. It's too near the house for comfort. I had a perfect right to lay poison. What do you want me to do—compensate McIver for the loss? That dog was pretty old, anyway. And it should never have been allowed to run wild on Falconsgarth land."

Somehow I couldn't imagine poor Maidie running wild over anyone's land. She was too old and placid for that. But at least I knew it had not been done deliberately.

"Peter . . . " I began again.

"Yes, Romaine?" His glance caressed my face, ran over my hair, his eyes alight with tender amusement.

Flushing under that intent gaze, I went on, "Why is Connan McIver our enemy?"

"Who said he was?"

"Grandmother did."

"Ah, I see. You like that old man, don't you? I have a feeling you like everyone. Even that old man's son?"

"Tom? He and I have hardly said two polite words to each other, and don't change the subject. Why did grandmother say Connan McIver hates us? He said he worked for grandfather for thirty years . . . "

"True enough. For grandfather and great-grandfather. But he was lazy. The sheep were doing very badly, so grandmother sacked him. You'll agree that an employer has a right to get rid of an employee who isn't pulling his weight."

"I suppose so," I said dubiously, reminding myself that I really knew very little about Connan McIver.

Peter reached out and laid a lock of my hair behind my shoulder. "He wasn't very pleased, of course. He refused to

move out of his cottage, though it was tied, so eventually
grandmother had to get the bailiffs in. That's when he moved
in with the Jamiesons, right on our doorstep, and he's been
out to get us ever since. You may find it hard to believe, but
it's the truth. Ask grandmother."

"Oh, I believe you," I said.

For a while we drank tea in silence. When he asked me for
another cup I automatically knelt by the table to pour it, which
made Peter grin to himself. I saw it, but my thoughts were
back on The Wood, so I didn't react.

"Peter . . ."

Smiling, he shook his head at me. "What is this? Question
time in the House? Do you know when you say my name
that way it sends shivers up my spine?" In one swift movement, he knelt beside me, one arm around me and the other
hand raising my face to his. "In fact, just looking at you
does peculiar things to me."

He kissed me, very slowly and expertly, and I was helpless, the teapot in one hand and the strainer in the other. If I
had moved I would have stained someone's clothes with tea.
But the instant he released my mouth I struggled free, protesting, "You'll make me spill it! Peter!"

"All right," he sighed, smiling into my eyes before
putting himself back on the settee. "But stop asking questions. Let me ask one instead—Have you got a boy-friend
in Paris, or anywhere else?"

"It depends what you mean by 'boy-friend'. I have friends
who are men—Stefan, Jean-Paul, Pierre . . ."

"But no one special?"

"They're all special, in different ways."

"Romaine! You know what I mean."

My nerves were still jolting uncomfortably and I was
tempted to lie in self-defence, but I refrained. "Yes. You mean
am I in love. Well, I'm not, nor do I intend to be, not yet.
Here's your tea."

"You can't decide when to fall in love," Peter reminded
me. "It just happens."

"Has it happened to you?" I asked, seating myself in an arm-chair.

He glanced at the place beside him, amused that I should be avoiding him. "It's too soon to be sure," he said meaningfully.

Fortunately, that was the moment when grandmother and aunt Lydia came in, both complaining of the cold. Grandmother sank into the chair opposite mine, while aunt Lydia sat beside her son.

"There isn't much tea left," I said, lifting the pot.

Grandmother waved a weary hand in the air. "That's no matter, Romaine. Amy's making a fresh pot. Oh, it's good to sit down in the warm. But the flowers look very nice, don't they, Lydia? Gerald used to like flowers about the place. I hope you'll come with us to the service, Romaine. We like to go as a family, at least this once a year."

"Of course," I said. "I'd love to."

When I had recovered from the rigours of the afternoon, I felt that I ought to visit the McIvers and tell them they had misunderstood the tragedy of Maidie's death. The evening was fine and it was not far to walk, but the problem was how to get away without telling the family where I was going, for I was sure they would not approve. When I commented that it was a pleasant evening for a walk, grandmother said I had done quite enough walking for one day and should sit quietly, or go to bed and read. It was clear that there was no way I could get out of the house that night.

All the same, I was anxious that the matter should be set right. The entire feud might be based on similar misunderstandings.

Standing at my window that night, drawn to stare at The Wood by some morbid fascination, I realised that the light I had seen the previous night must have been carried by Tom as he searched for the dog. The thought made me laugh to myself, in relief. Imagine being scared by a torch, or a lantern, especially when Tom accompanied it. I wished I had remembered in time to tell him. He would have laughed, too.

No, he wouldn't. Idiot, Romaine. Tom Jamieson would have sneered at your fantasies, as he sneers at your family. Remember how he assaulted you, only yesterday?

My fingers moved over my lips, remembering. Two men had kissed me, one angrily, one sensually, and it was hard to decide which had offended me more. Not that it mattered. I had no intention of letting either of them get that close again. Red roses from a florist, tiny blue petals on a speedwell ... I wished now that I had accepted Tom's peace offering.

Despite these late thoughts, it was not of Tom or Peter that I dreamed, but of uncle Walter. In the morning I could not recall any details of the dream, but my face was stiff with dried tears.

Since this was a special occasion for the family, we travelled to church in the thirty-year-old Rolls Royce, which was brought out of its garage only rarely. Grandmother and aunt Lydia were both dressed in black, which made the one look elegant and the other merely plain. My uncle and cousin, too, were sombrely dressed, making me feel conspicuous in my oatmeal dress and jacket. But I did not possess a black outfit—the colour looked appalling with my dark hair and olive skin.

The organ was being played very softly as we entered the church a minute or two before ten-thirty. A murmur went round the congregation and heads turned, some of the gazes fixed curiously on me and others cold and set, sending out waves of hostility that astounded me.

Seated beside aunt Lydia in the front pew, I found myself praying incoherently for guidance and protection against the forces of evil which I sensed at Falconsgarth, and against the hatred I could feel inside the church. What was the cause of it? Did the entire village hate the Faulkners? Why?

The vicar proved to be a youngish man, a little overweight but pleasant-looking, with a smiling round face beneath thinning hair. His theme was Sacrifice, which blended well with the Remembrance Day sentiments and also managed to cover

some of the things my grandfather had done for the village—
such as paying for the repair of the church roof.

"And giving the hall to the W.I.," a voice breathed
hoarsely from directly behind me. I felt aunt Lydia stiffen,
but she didn't look round and neither did I. The significance
of the highly-charged remark was a mystery to me.

When the service ended we were again obliged to brave
the glances of the villagers as they remained in their places
while we moved towards the door. It was horribly feudal and
I was glad when we turned behind the last pew.

"An excellent sermon, vicar," grandmother congratulated
the young clergyman who stood in the porch shaking hands.
"I hope you liked the flowers. Oh, Romaine . . . My dear, this
is Reverend Bland. My grand-daughter, vicar."

His grip was firm as he said, "How do you do. I'm
delighted to meet you, Miss Faulkner," and I murmured
something in reply.

"We'll see you at lunch," grandmother reminded him as
we departed. "Twelve-thirty for one. Don't be late."

"Oh, indeed I shan't, Lady Faulkner," he assured her
with a grin.

As the Rolls moved smoothly away, I saw the first member
of the rest of the congregation come through the lych gate,
almost as if our neighbours were deliberately avoiding us.

"Hypocrites!" aunt Lydia muttered under her breath.

"What's the W.I.?" I asked. "The Women's . . . "

"Institute!" my aunt hissed in my face, so viciously that
I recoiled and bumped my head on the side cushions of the
car, not daring to ask the next obvious question as to the
meaning of the whisper in church.

Back at Falconsgarth, Amy had coffee waiting. It was only
then that I remembered I had been hoping to have a private
word with Tom Jamieson after the service, but I had not
noticed him in church—not that I had cared to search too
closely for fear of meeting hostile eyes.

"I think I'll go for a walk before lunch," I announced.

"Haven't you done enough for one morning?" grandmother asked. "Evan Bland will be here in half an hour, you know."

"Besides, it looks like rain," my aunt added.

I glanced out of the window, where above the trees the sky was a pure washed blue with only a few wisps of cloud.

"Nonsense, mother," Peter returned, joining me. "If Romaine wants to stretch her legs, I'll go with her. A gentle constitutional will do us both good. And don't worry. We'll be back in good time to exchange pleasantries over sherry with Evan Bland. Coming, Romaine?"

Cursing my luck, I smiled brightly and concurred, though I could hardly go to the McIvens' cottage with Peter tagging along. Instead we took a brief stroll through the woods, circling the house, while Peter flirted with me and I fended him off, laughingly but firmly.

We returned to find the vicar arrived early, sipping sherry in the big blue and gold drawing room with grandmother and aunt Lydia. Uncle Walter was there, too, having been chivvied out of his hidey-hole behind the library, though he was being ignored and looking unhappy, as usual.

"Cheer up!" I urged as I joined him. "It's not that bad, is it?"

His smile was infinitely sad. "Isn't it? No, you're right, of course. Nothing is ever as bad as it seems. Isn't that what they say? I can almost believe it, since you came. You've brought a little brightness back into my life, for which I'm grateful."

"Flatterer," I teased. "I must say the Faulkner men are charming. Peter's been laying it on thick, too."

"Has he?" He flicked a worried glance in his son's direction, saying under his breath, "I wish you'd never come, Romaine."

"But you just said . . ."

"I know what I said!" The lemonade in his glass splashed with his agitation. "Oh, take no notice. I ramble. I wish to God I could have a drink! No, I don't mean that, either. Oh,

Romaine, get away from here. Go away before you get tarnished."

Before I could think of a reply to that bewildering directive, Peter was approaching with Evan Bland in tow.

"Father?" was all he said to uncle Walter, who ducked away muttering an excuse.

My cousin laid an arm around my shoulders, saying in a confidential tone, "Evan here is dying to have words with you. Not that I blame him. This village is full of moor ponies and you're a thoroughbred. And Evan is on the look-out for a wife to tend that draughty old vicarage of his. Aren't you, Evan?"

The vicar blushed to his ears, denying any such intentions.

"Anyway," Peter added, "you'll have to join the queue. I saw her first. And there's . . . who was it, Romaine?"

"You mean Jean-Paul, Stefan, and Pierre?"

"Ah." He frowned into my face. "They do exist, do they?"

"Every one of them," I said levelly, moving aside so that he had to remove his arm from around me. "How long have you been in Winterford, Mr. Bland? Is that right—it is correct to call you Mister?"

"I'd prefer it if you call me Evan, as your cousin does," he replied with a smile. "And I've been in Winterford for two years."

"Small-talk," Peter groaned, laughing over his shoulder as he went to refill his glass.

He was probably right about the quality of the conversation, but it was pleasant and we soon felt at ease, Evan and I, as if we had known each other for years. Despite Peter's teasing remarks it was soon evident that there was no personal attraction between the young vicar and myself, and with sex dispensed with we were able to be friends. Neither of us was a threat to the other, in any way.

It was this easiness which made me feel that perhaps Evan was the person to talk to about my inner struggle over The

Wood. The subject could hardly be raised with the family around us, but I asked if I might talk to him privately one day soon.

"Privately?" He sounded surprised. "Why . . . why, yes, of course. . . ."

"It's all right, Evan, I have no designs on your vicarage," I said drily. "It's a personal matter—personal to me, that is. Let's say I'm in two minds about something and I need your advice."

"I'd be only too delighted. Any time. Except Tuesdays and Thursdays. I'm in school then. Teaching part-time. Mentally sub-normal children, you know."

"You must be a very nice man," I said sincerely, and he laughed and blushed, offering me his arm as we went in to lunch.

It was during the afternoon that I began to suspect I was being watched. Everywhere I went, Peter followed me. He said he was at a loose end and wanted company of his own generation on his one free day, but even when I returned from a visit to the bathroom he was hovering by the stairs.

"Why don't we go out for a drive?" he asked.

"I have some letters to write," I replied. "I started one yesterday and didn't finish it."

"Oh? A letter to whom?"

"To my friend Marie-Elise, if it's any business of yours," I said, losing my patience. "Peter, haven't you any friends of your own? Don't you ever go out?"

"Of course I do, but . . . I want to be with you. Isn't that obvious? You can write your letters tomorrow, when I'm working. Please, Romaine! We can have dinner out, if you like. There's a new place opened on the Taunton road which does a fantastic steak."

I almost capitulated, but a spark of common sense prevented me. It was pointless to encourage Peter when the attraction was all on his side, flattering though it was. "I really don't feel like dressing up. Not tonight Peter. At the end of the day I still feel very tired."

His face twisted with anger. "You'd have gone if Evan had asked you."

"Don't be ridiculous!"

"Or Tom Jamieson," he added. "You go for the rough type, do you?"

"You're being very tiresome," I said. "Excuse me, I'm going to the library to write letters."

Before I had written two sentences, Peter came in saying he wasn't going to disturb me, he wanted to read the newspapers in peace and quiet. Setting himself in a leather armchair beneath the portrait of General Sir Gerald, he did just that, with much rustling of pages and under-breath exclamations. I found myself telling Marie-Elise jokingly about this cousin who was so besotted with me he couldn't leave me alone for a minute, but in truth I was less than amused. It seemed that I would not have a chance to visit the McIvers until the following day.

Determined not to be bested in this way, I retired early to my room after dinner and sat reading until a reasonable time had passed. It was nearly ten o'clock when I ventured out and silently closed the door.

The house was quiet. I had left the family in the television room watching a film, which would be ending soon. With any luck they would all be too engrossed to leave before the end, so the only people I might meet were uncle Walter and Amy.

However, I met no one as I made my way through the passages to the rear door, which had already been locked for the night. I turned the key softly, hoping that no one would check the door before I returned. Usually the family did not go to bed until around midnight, so I had two hours in which to complete my mission.

Outside, a fitful moon showed between windy clouds, but it was too dark to go through the woods. I circled the house, walking on the grass for quietness, and gained the drive without mishap, hearing the trees muttering around me. I stopped, alarmed, when the owl hooted softly from somewhere to my right, mocking me, reminding me of the pale form swooping across the front of the house the previous day, in clear warning. Was I walking into danger by going to the cottage? No, I couldn't believe that.

Taking the narrow lane which skirted the high wall of Falconsgarth, I moved more easily, but not fast enough to make the pain in my side stab. Soon I came to the road which ran up into the hills and from there it was only a minute before I saw a lighted window ahead of me.

As I reached the cottage, another light sprang up behind curtains on the upper floor, but when I knocked on the door it was soon opened, by Tom Jamieson. He stared at me as if I were a Martian.

" I know it's late," I said. " I couldn't get away before, but I had to come. Is Mr. McIver here?"

" He's just gone to bed," he replied brusquely, glancing at the sturdy watch on his wrist. " Couldn't it have waited until morning?"

" Well, yes, I suppose . . ." It could have waited, I thought, surprised at myself. Why had I bothered to sneak out when in the morning I could have ' gone for a walk ' and nobody would have known? Except that I had tried that ruse already and been prevented.

" You'd better come in," Tom said, opening the door wider.

The sitting-room smelled of apples. There were boxes of them, wrapped in paper ready to be stored. A coal fire burned low in a tiled grate around which a suite covered in green moquette was grouped.

Behind me in the hall I heard Tom talking softly to Connan McIver, but I made for the fire and stood warming my hands, looking at the ornaments which decorated the mantelpiece. It was a homely place, clean but not repressively tidy, and there was peace here underlying any surface moods, where at Falconsgarth there was always that unease which made my nerves watchful.

Tom reappeared and stood by the door straightening his

sweater over lean hips, eyes narrowed. "Con won't be long. This had better be important."

"It is! At least . . . it seemed important to me. I want to set the record straight. There seem to be so many misunderstandings . . . "

"About what?"

"About all sorts of things," I said lamely. "We're neighbours, Tom. Isn't it time we stopped this silly feud?"

His eyebrows lifted and he slowly let out his breath in disbelief, walking towards me in a leisurely fashion. "I don't know whether to admire your nerve or wonder at your innocence. Do you seriously think you can come here, a total stranger, and set right all the wrongs that have been done over fifty years?"

"Not all of them, no. I don't pretend to know the whole story, but this one thing . . . "

"What thing is that?" the old man's voice said heavily from the doorway. He must have dressed hastily for half of his shirt collar stuck out from the neck of a baggy sweater, and his hair and beard were rumpled.

"It's about Maidie," I said. "Mr. McIver, I can't tell you how sorry we all are for what happened." That was an exaggeration—I was sorry, but I wasn't so sure about the rest of the family. "I know how fond of her you must have been. It must have been awful to see her . . . "

"It was." His voice was quiet, but there was kindness in his look.

Beside me, Tom threw out his arms in an angry gesture. "You're surely not going to listen to this, Con. She's been sent to soften you up."

"I wasn't sent!" I exclaimed. "I came of my own free will, without anyone else knowing. I wanted you to understand . . . Mr. McIver, Tom said my family deliberately killed your dog, but it isn't true! Peter had that poison put down for rats. He told me so."

"Rats!" Tom almost shouted, his eyes glowing with fury.

"Be quiet, Tom," the old man's voice came, low but firm. "Can't you see she's telling the truth—as she knows it? Romaine . . . sit down, please. By the fire. We must talk about this."

Unwillingly, I sank into the armchair, resentment against Tom Jamieson burning inside me. He remained standing, thumbs thrust aggressively into his belt, while Connan limped slowly to the settee and lowered his great bulk with a sigh.

"There are rats in The Wood, you see," I told him. "Peter never intended for Maidie to be hurt. You must believe that."

"I believe that *you* believe it," Connan said. "How much do you know about rats, Romaine?"

"Very little, I'm thankful to say."

"But you know they're scavengers, they exist on scraps. So they live close to man, in sewers, cellars and barns. What would they find to live on in The Wood?"

His blue eyes were steady on mine and I could think of no answer.

Connan leaned on his knees, staring at me sorrowfully. "Your cousin lied to you, Romaine. There are no rats in that wood. As far as I know, there never have been. Wood mice, maybe. Hedgehogs and squirrels, maybe even a fox. But not rats."

"Oh, you never know," Tom put in with sarcasm. "Perhaps there's a new breed of hippy rats—who've dropped out of the rat-race."

I felt bewildered and scarcely heard the facetious remark, but Connan smiled gently at me.

"Tom's angry on my account, you see. If it was for himself he wouldn't be so touchy with you, but he seems to think I need protection."

"And so you do!" Tom raged. "Though God knows what we can possibly do against that lot. I hope they do cut down those trees. I hope the curse comes true!"

"Tom!"

Now the old man was angry and I, too, looked up at Tom, a hand to my throat. I suppose I was wide-eyed and pale, showing my fear, for his expression softened as he added, " Oh, not you. I don't include you. Just the rest of them."

" They're still my family, Tom," I managed.

" But they lied to you," he reminded me.

" Not all of them. And Peter . . . he must have had reason to think there were rats. He wouldn't set out to poison a dog. It's so . . . petty and cruel. What good has it done?"

" It has hurt Con," was Tom's explanation.

I stood up, unable to think straight, and found myself trembling. " I must go, before they check the door. They told me I mustn't see you. I'm sorry to have disturbed you."

" Wait until I get my jacket," Tom instructed. " I'll walk you back."

" There's really no need."

His eyes held mine, grey and sombre. " There's every need," he said quietly.

FIVE

All the clouds had gone and in the pale moonlight frost was beginning to sparkle. We used the back gate of the cottage, onto the hillside, intending to skirt the woods until we were at a point opposite Falconsgarth. When I stumbled in the uneven grass, Tom caught my hand to prevent my falling and kept hold of it, guiding my feet with his torch.

" I saw you up on the hill the other night," I said through teeth that wanted to chatter with the cold. " At least, I saw the light. It frightened me to death. My father used to tell me about a phantom light that appeared on May eve, and for a minute I thought I'd seen it."

" I'm sorry," Tom said. " It was a lamp I had—when I was looking for Maidie."

"Yes, I thought so. After you told me about Maidie . . . Oh, Tom, Peter wouldn't have done it on purpose! He wouldn't!"

He paused briefly to look at me in the moonlight. " I would like to believe that. I really would. Maybe I'm prejudiced, but I have good reason to be. This isn't the first little nastiness that's happened, it's just the latest."

Knowing we would never agree on the matter, I didn't argue further but clutched my jacket more closely round my neck. The cold was biting my face and numbing my nose, the only warmth coming from the firm hand that was held tightly round mine, as we took a diagonal course through the woods. The downward slope was littered with crisp leaves and twigs, forcing us to move slowly.

At last we reached the edge of the woods and Falconsgarth reared before us. The moonlight made patterns on the ivy and spread across the sloping lawn where every grass-blade was edged with silver.

" I can manage now," I breathed. " Thank you for coming with me. Good night."

" Good night." He released my hand, but as I moved away he spoke my name softly, for the first time calling me " Romaine?"

Beneath the shadow of a tree, I looked over my shoulder. " Yes?"

" When the roses come, ignore the note. I might have meant it then, but I don't mean it now."

" Roses?" I said blankly, peering through the chequered darkness where he was little more than a shadow, the torch out now.

" You probably don't remember, but I said something snide the other day about a dozen red roses being required—before you would accept an apology."

He waited for me to reply, but I was so surprised I could think of nothing to say.

"Anyway, I ordered some," Tom went on awkwardly. "I went into town that same afternoon. And I'm afraid I wrote a sarcastic note to go with them. They'll probably arrive tomorrow, or Tuesday. Only ... forget the note, will you?"

"Why, what does it say?"

"I'd rather not tell you. Do me a favour and tear it up while it's still sealed in the envelope."

I was puzzled by the coincidence of *two* gifts of red roses. "Tom ... where did you order the flowers?"

"Hathersage's. Why?"

"Nothing, really. I had a dozen red roses from Peter on Saturday. They were from Hathersage's, too. A whole vanful came—to decorate the church."

"Oh," Tom said, his voice curiously flat. "Coals to Newcastle, then."

"Not at all," I replied softly. "I love roses."

There was a moment's breathless silence, then a twig cracked beneath his shoes as he moved towards me in the darkness. "Maybe I ought to make sure you can get in. Don't they lock the doors at night?"

"Yes, but I unlocked the back door, so unless they've noticed ... "

"Let's find out," he said, and took my hand again.

I felt like a naughty child returning from a scrumping raid as we crunched across the frosty grass in the moonlight and came to the door among the ivy. The knob was cold beneath my hand. It turned, but the door would not open.

"*Zut!*" I muttered.

"What?" said Tom.

"Ssssh! It's a swear word. The door's locked." I had an insane desire to giggle, because the whole thing had suddenly become absurd. "What am I going to do?"

"Can't you just knock?"

"I'm supposed to be in bed. How can I explain what I'm doing out here—especially with you? Oh, I know—keep your fingers crossed that uncle Walter's still in the study. He'll let me in."

With Tom in tow, I stole silently round a shadowy buttress and saw with relief that there was still a light behind the heavy curtains of the study, which lay at the corner of the house.

"That's good," I breathed. "You can go now, Tom. Don't let uncle Walter see you with me."

"Why not?"

"Because . . . I told you—I've been instructed to stay away from your family. It's mad and I intend to change it, but not now."

"I'm not afraid of Walter," Tom assured me. "Anyway, if you're going through that window you'll need a hand up. Except . . ." As he paused, he laid his hand on my wrist, preventing me from knocking on the window, and when I looked up in surprise our eyes met questioningly. He was very close to me, his breath warm on my cheek.

"I'm sorry for the things I've said," he told me quietly.

"You're forgiven," I said, equally softly. "Tom . . ."

And he kissed me, very gently, full on my unresisting lips, making a quirk of excitement twist inside me. Without another word, he stepped past me and himself tapped on the leaded window.

A moment later the curtains were drawn back and uncle Walter looked out, blinking at us in astonishment before opening the window wide. A gust of warm air and cigarette smoke rushed out.

"Romaine! Tom . . . what on earth is going on?"

"I've been playing truant," I confessed, "and got myself locked out. Can I climb through the window?"

"You can try, I suppose. Girl, you're crazy!"

Tom's firm hands closed round my waist and a moment later I was sitting on the window sill, my head reeling crazily.

"When shall I see you again?" Tom asked.

"Oh, for goodness' sake!" uncle Walter sighed. "Couldn't you have arranged all that before you got me to open the window? It's freezing in here. Come back at eight tomorrow night, Tom. If Romaine isn't here, she'll give me a message for you. Come on, girl."

It had been a silly, school-girl escapade and when I half-fell into the room I wrenched my scarred ribs, but somehow I didn't care.

My uncle pulled the chair from behind his desk and set it near the radiator, putting me into it before himself leaning on his desk, lighting a cigarette.

"You won't tell on me, will you?" I said, hugging the radiator.

He shook his head. "You remind me too much of myself, unfortunately. Haven't you been warned that Tom and his family are sworn enemies?"

Something about his voice made me stare at him. He sounded almost cynical.

"You don't believe that, either, do you?" I said.

But the moment of rebellion was past. He turned away from me, sighing "I don't know what I believe any more. All I want is a quiet life. You'd better get to bed. If you meet anyone, say you've been with me all evening. I haven't seen a soul since dinner, so they can't prove otherwise. Better leave your coat here."

I did as I was bid, the euphoria draining away to leave me depressed. Perhaps it was the aura of evil that lay over Falconsgarth which affected me, but I still had my memories of a short freedom, a scent of apples, and Tom's warmth in the cold night.

"Well, Romaine!"

The voice startled me and I whirled round to see Peter coming from the passage which led to the back door.

"I thought you were in bed," he said, his eyes asking questions.

"I got delayed—in the study with your father, looking at the albums. We forgot the time." I yawned ostentatiously. "Goodness, yes. It's suddenly caught up with me. Good night, Peter."

As I climbed the stairs I was aware of his eyes on me every

step of the way and a shiver that was not caused by cold ran up my spine. Did Peter suspect that I had been out? Why should it matter to him, except that he was becoming obsessively jealous? It was horrible to be checked on as if I were a criminal, or an idiot. In the morning I would tell them where I had been, and ask for the truth about the poison—and about the roses. That was something else which didn't quite fit.

In the morning, of course, I did nothing of the kind. Peter had gone to work and grandmother smiled benevolently on me. It was crazy to think of rat poison and lies; so I behaved as though nothing had happened.

I did, however, try to find the green box which the roses had come in, only to be told by Amy that she had burned all the rubbish on Saturday afternoon, the box among it. So if Tom's 'sarcastic' note had fallen in with the wrappings, it, too, would be burnt—except, I reminded myself, that the flowers had been from Peter. Another florist's box would arrive, that day or the next, proving the incident to be an amazing coincidence and nothing more.

Over lunch, unseen by the others, uncle Walter winked and gestured at me to meet him in the study afterwards, which I did.

"I just want to ask you to do me a favour, Romaine," he said, checking that the library was empty before closing the study door. "Those pictures ought to be ready by now. I'd rather not fetch them myself, in case . . . well, it means explanations and argument. But you could go. You're a one for walks."

"You're not a prisoner, are you?" I asked, a little irritated by his meek acceptance of the treatment he received from his family.

"Yes, virtually. Oh, I know what you think. I used to fight it, too, but after a while your spirit breaks. It's easier this way. And I do want to see those pictures. Tomorrow they're coming to start felling The Wood."

Although that seemed not to follow what he had been saying earlier, it was alarming enough to make me ignore the inconsistency. "Tomorrow?"

"It should have been today, but they've hit some snag. Mother's furious. But after all this time one day won't make much difference."

"And neither will the felling of that Wood!" I said, too firmly, denying all my darker instincts.

"Well, we shall soon see. In a few days there'll be nothing left to argue about, one way or another. Will you fetch the pictures?"

"Yes. We can put them in the album this evening, then if Tom comes . . . " A little chirrup of brightness lightened the gloom inside me. "See you later."

Taking the jacket I had left in the study the previous night, I made for the front door, only to encounter a heavily-aproned aunt Lydia. In her hands she was carrying a salver piled with items of the family silver.

"Ransacking the place?" I asked lightly.

"Don't be childish!" she retorted. "And where are you going, may I ask?"

"For a walk. I won't be long."

"A walk to where?"

My hand on the front door-knob, I turned with an irritable remark on my lips, only to be stopped by the sight of grandmother standing at the foot of the stairs. I did not like to be rude to my aunt in front of my sweetly-smiling grandmother.

"I'm going to the vicarage to see Evan Bland," I replied. "I want to talk to him—about a religious matter, strange as it may seem."

Grandmother advanced, nodding her white head. "It's not strange at all, Romaine. I'm sure Evan will be delighted to see you. Lydia . . . didn't you say you wanted to go to the shops? Why don't you drive Romaine to the vicarage? It will save her a walk both ways. You must really take things more easily, Romaine. I shan't be happy until you're glowing with health."

"I feel better every day," I told her.

"Well, you don't show it, my dear. You're all hollow round

the eyes. Lydia, take those things to the kitchen and bring
the car keys."

My aunt looked askance at her burdens, which she had
obviously been about to polish, but said, " Yes, mother," and
departed.

" If it comes to that," I remarked to grandmother, " I can
drive myself, if you don't mind my borrowing the car."

Her pale, almost translucent hand fell on my arm. " But
Lydia has some shopping to do. Don't be too long at the
vicarage, will you? I worry about you, you know."

She waited with me until aunt Lydia returned, wearing
a top coat and a sour expression. Hardly bothering even to
speak to me, she drove me through the village to the top of
the High Street and pointed out to me the vicarage, which
lay down a weed-grown driveway beside the churchyard.

The breeze was still chilly, but the sun was shining and the
birds singing as though they thought it was spring. I walked
down the drive towards the rambling brick house behind a
row of elms, and half way there something made me look
round. My aunt was still sitting in the car watching me, but
when I waved she drove off—away from the shops. It was
only then that I became sure that I was being watched, my
movements checked on. Yesterday, and now today, I had not
been able to move without someone coming with me. Where
on earth did they think I might go?

To the McIvers', the answer came. The family were
determined to keep me away from Connan, Ruth and Tom.
I was entirely sure that grandmother had sent Lydia to
make certain that I was going to the vicarage and no-
where else.

The finger of darkness touched me again and I looked up
to where the trees on the knoll were just visible from that
angle. *Why* was I being so closely watched? Was it, as grandmother claimed, for my own protection?

There were rooks in the elms, making a terrible racket in
the cold afternoon as I passed beneath a branch archway and
approached the vicarage, still feeling uncomfortable about

being spied on. The house had a sad, neglected air, though it was not as old as most of the houses in the village.

"Good afternoon!" Evan's voice hailed me, from above. He was perched on a ladder, up by the eaves at the corner of the house. "Hang on a minute and I'll be with you."

Digging into the guttering, he sent a clod of some indescribable filth to spatter into the flower border, then nimbly came down the ladder and held out slimey black hands.

"Hardly the garb to greet a lady, but the thing leaked last time it rained. Since I can't afford to pay someone to do it, I must be my own handyman. Do you mind coming round the back way? There's some heat on in the kitchen."

The garden was mainly threadbare grass, with an old swing rusting in the far corner by the low wall. I was surprised to see that the river ran beyond the wall, curving off into the distance between the hills; so I could easily get from here to the mill along the river bank, later.

"Do sit down," Evan invited, scrubbing his hands under the cold tap. "I'll put the kettle on and we'll have a cup of coffee. Sorry it's not an elegant drawing room like you have at Falconsgarth, but ..."

"This suits me fine," I said, sitting at the scrubbed wooden table, in a chair that felt none too steady. "You should see my garret in Paris. My kitchen is a fraction the size of this."

"But cheap to heat, no doubt," Evan replied with a rueful glance around the huge, stone-flagged room. Plastic matting covered areas of the floor and an oil heater struggled valiantly against the draughts. I didn't even think of removing my jacket.

Having made two mugs of instant coffee, Evan sat opposite me, smoothing his thin fair hair. He was wearing two sweaters, the outer one streaked with paint, and his square hands looked raw with the cold.

"This is a real pleasure," he said with a smile, "though I hardly expected you so soon. It must be important."

"It seems to be, though now I'm here ... Evan, you'll think I'm crazy."

" I very much doubt it." There was kindness and concern in his brown eyes. " Just say it, whatever it is. I'll do anything I can to help."

I twisted the coffee mug on the table, slowly turning it round and round, my eyes glued on it. " Do you believe in the Devil?"

" The Devil?" He was caught by surprise and took his time to consider his answer carefully. " As a Christian, of course, I know there is a God. Therefore, there may also be His opposite, though I can't think of the Devil as having equal powers. Why do you ask?"

Pulling my mouth awry, I glanced up at him. " Because I'm beset by doubts. I keep telling myself it's self-delusion—my Romany heritage and mother's weird premonitions—but at other times I actually do believe . . . I suppose you've heard about the legend—The Wood on the hill, linked with my family?"

" Oh, that. Yes. Actually I came across some old maps in the vestry soon after I arrived. It . . . " He stopped himself so suddenly that I lifted my head and saw him looking troubled.

" It what?"

" After your earlier question, perhaps I'm wrong to tell you, but The Wood, as people now call it, was once Devil's Wood, on the maps. Romaine, it *is* just a legend. I have heard that a man was killed by lightning when he attempted to cut one of the trees, but that is just coincidence."

" Is it coincidence that my father died about the same time?"

He stared at me worriedly. " Did he? I didn't know."

" Six years and two months ago. That's how Connan McIver puts it."

" Ah! Mr. McIver." He leapt on the name with evident relief. " I might have known he would be somewhere behind this. He holds some very strange beliefs. I don't doubt he can read the weather and the signs of nature, but the rest . . . Whatever he's told you, don't take it too seriously. You're a Christian, aren't you?"

" I like to think so. At least, half of me is. The other half
...I feel something evil at Falconsgarth, Evan. I feel it
through my pores and my nerves, in my bones and my sub-
conscious. It's there, hanging over the house like an invisible
black cloud. And the other day, in the church, I felt ... oh,
I can't describe it. I felt the threat of danger, very strongly.
Or am I imagining things?"

Evan was silent for a moment, watching me closely. " Is
that what you want me to tell you? Only you can decide that,
Romaine. Let me say this—there is a force for Good, that
much I know, and there may be a force for Evil. But it is
not a living entity with power to bring down lightning and
harm the innocent. The Devil can only work in men's
minds."

"And you think I'm possessed," I said flatly. " Three
hundred years ago, I would have been hanged as a witch,
like one of my ancestors."

His smile was gentle, amused. " Three hundred years ago
there was a lot of ignorance about. Think of it logically,
Romaine. What evil can there possibly be at Falconsgarth?"

" There's The Wood. Tomorrow they come to cut it.
Grandmother is defying the curse, as she did once before ..."

" I said logically," he reminded me.

I drank the cooling coffee, sipping it as I mentally re-
viewed the facts. Lies there had been, about rat poison and
perhaps about roses; retribution there certainly was, witness
poor uncle Walter; and surveillance there was, on my movements particularly, for reasons I did not care to examine too
closely.

On the other hand, it was possible that Peter might
genuinely have thought The Wood was infested by rats; that
Tom's roses would arrive tomorrow; perhaps the family were
right not to trust uncle Walter; and their watching of me
might be simply out of concern for my well-being.

" You see?" Evan said kindly when I made no reply to his
question. " I don't doubt there are human frailties at Falconsgarth, as there are in every household. But evil? No, Romaine.

I can't believe that, and neither should you, for your own sake. Have some more coffee?"

"No, thank you." I gave him a quick smile and stood up, hands deep in my jacket pockets. "I'll let you get back to your gutters. But thank you for listening to me, Evan."

"Any time." He escorted me to the door, letting the cold sunlight slant into the room. "Just don't forget that you've been through a traumatic time recently. Your mother, and your own injuries . . . It's bound to have taken its toll, mentally as well as physically."

"Yes, I expect you're right." He was telling me as kindly as he could that my head was full of cotton wool. "Do you mind if I climb over your wall? I'd like to walk by the river."

Evan looked ruefully at the low structure. "You can go through it, by those trees. It's falling down, I'm afraid. Goodbye, Romaine."

We shook hands and I parted from him, aware that my talk with him had not helped me at all. He obviously held orthodox views, but to me the feeling of evil was very real, though I had not explained it very well. It was not something which could be put into words: it was intangible. But so were love and hatred, and no one denied the reality of those emotions.

The thought of what might happen when the men came to fell the trees lay over my mind like a dark shadow, clouding the crisp sunlight and the sparkle of the river, but I made a conscious effort to dismiss it. Think logically, Evan had said. Logically, trees were only trees.

There was a battered old jalopy of uncertain colour parked outside the mill, and when I climbed the steps and knocked the door was opened by a big, bald-headed man wearing glasses that enlarged his blue eyes. He had a pronounced stoop of his shoulders, as if he were trying to disguise his height, but his smile was wide and toothy.

"Don't tell me! You're Romaine Faulkner and you've come for the pictures. I'd have known you anywhere. You're very photogenic."

" Stop flirting and shut the door," Jill's voice came drily from inside the mill, and Dick let me in, grinning.

The room was in the same cheerful disarray, except that Jill was sitting in a low chair with the baby at her breast. The other two children sprawled on the floor apparently making confetti of magazines.

" Have a seat," Dick suggested, pulling a chair round next to Jill for me. " I'll get the photos. Couldn't Walter get away from the dragons?"

" I don't think he wanted to take a chance," I said.

" Hag-ridden," was Jill's word for it as she laid the baby against her shoulder, patting its back. " That poor man . . . Hasn't he been punished enough without them constantly reminding him of his sins? Oh, it's none of my business, I know. Dick's always telling me I'm an interfering busybody. But I'm very fond of Walter."

" Yes, so am I," I said.

Her husband re-appeared from gloomy regions at the back of the room, bringing a large envelope which he was tapping thoughtfully against a long thumb-nail, whistling between his teeth. " They've come out well," he informed me. " You'd better have a look."

It was only when I took the photographs from the envelope that I remembered my uncle had finished a film with only four shots. The other six were new to me—pictures of The Wood, of Connan McIver with Maidie at his feet, and one of Tom, smiling as he leaned on the cottage gate. The sight made me smile, too, though I was puzzled by these pictures which uncle Walter had taken. Was he more friendly with the McIvers than he dared to admit to me?

The two frames of myself against the woods were not bad, though I wished afresh that my Uncle had smiled when I took his photograph, for he looked terribly solemn. Lastly there was the final shot of me, and as I looked at it I caught my breath in horror, for behind my shoulder there was a face —a demoniac face with horns and a long tongue. I blinked to clear my eyes, disbelievingly, and in the background of the picture there was the ivy on the wall. It was only ivy.

"You saw it, didn't you?" Dick said eagerly.

I looked up at him standing beside me, though I didn't see him. "Saw what?"

"The mask, or whatever it is. It was quite clear as the picture developed, but when the ivy got darker it was obscured. Jill saw it, too. Do you mind if I keep the negative? I'm going to make a paler print, if I can."

"I'd rather you didn't," I got out, leaping to my feet. Suddenly I felt sick. This was another warning, and this time other people had seen it. It was a clear indication of malevolence, and it was directed at me. My strange dreams, the owl, the heavy feeling of oppression, the premonition in the church . . . it was a personal danger which faced me. Of that I was now sure.

I don't remember leaving the mill. I found myself wandering through the village, along a crooked lane I had never seen before, where cottages leaned together, close against the road. They seemed to be trying to hem me in and I felt as though I could not breathe the air that had turned colder as clouds obscured the sun.

Then there was open space behind iron railings and I paused there, realising that I must have been running, stupidly, for pain seared through my chest. I had been panting, panicking, staring at the building beyond the railings for several minutes before my mind registered the stone in the wall on which was carved 'W.I.'. The place was a hall, not very large, roofed with corrugated iron. Someone in church had hissed something about a hall and the W.I., but at that moment I couldn't think clearly enough to pinpoint it.

As the pain subsided, allowing me to breathe more easily, I turned away from the hall, glancing round at the cottages in the hope that no one had witnessed my panic. And from a window across the lane a woman peered from the crack of a net curtain, staring at me with an expression that was ugly with hatred.

SIX

"Grandmother! You mustn't let them touch The Wood! You mustn't!"

Looking back, I find it hardly surprising that my hysterical outburst was greeted with shock and concern. I must have looked a sight—my hair dishevelled, my eyes wild, my face probably white from the knife of pain that lanced through my side. That few minutes remains a jumble in my mind because I was almost incoherent.

I do remember being forcibly taken to my room by aunt Lydia, with grandmother coming behind us. They helped me off with my coat and shoes and put me into bed, though I protested bitterly, and I recall aunt Lydia saying, " . . . same trouble with her father." There were pills, too, which grandmother said were tranquillisers. She stood over me until I had taken them, then sat on the bed stroking my hair, discussing with my aunt the advisability of calling the doctor.

"I really don't need a doctor!" I exclaimed. "It's only because I've been running. I'll be fine in a few minutes."

"Shush!" grandmother crooned, her hand soft and cool on my forehead. "You've got yourself upset over nothing. Just lie quietly, my dear. Lydia, will you ask Amy to bring a pot of tea for Romaine?"

Muttering, my aunt left the room.

Grandmother smiled at me. "Now, let us talk calmly. I thought you had agreed with me that the nonsense about The Wood was not worth even discussing. What has made

you change your mind? Surely Evan didn't say anything to
disturb you?"

"No, it wasn't Evan. It's just a feeling I have. I can't
explain it." I closed my eyes, defeated, because she would
not believe me, whatever I said. I should have known that.

"I know what the trouble is," grandmother said, her voice
soft with understanding. "You have listened to your father's
stories about that wood until you believe them, as he did. But
he was influenced by Mr. McIver, you know. Your father was
an impressionable boy." She paused, stroking my hair. "The
thing that I have always wondered, my dear, is what reason
there should be for connecting a stand of trees with the
family. Where did the story begin? No one seems to know
the answer. Like so many of these myths, it must have grown
and become confused with the passage of time. Of course it's
romantic, but there are more pleasant legends about this
family. Did you know that Beau Brummel once seduced a
Faulkner lady? Yes, that's what they say."

The gentle voice went on, talking persuasively, and my
eyelids drooped under the influence of the pills. She was right,
of course, I thought sleepily. I had allowed myself to forget
reason and be driven to panic. By what—a trick of light in a
photograph? Stupid, Romaine.

"I'll hang your jacket up," grandmother said, her weight
leaving the bed. "What's this, in your pocket?"

Horrified, I opened my eyes and saw that she was holding
the envelope with the photographs in it, but my brain was too
sluggish for me to lie convincingly.

"They're . . . only some pictures. I collected them
from . . ."

She was regarding my face with interest. "From Dick
Handley, you mean? My dear, exactly what has your uncle
been telling you? I suppose he said that I objected to his
friendship with the Handleys, did he? Yes, he would. Walter
. . ." She sighed, shaking her head. "Walter does like to
indulge in little mysteries. Really you are a gullible child,
Romaine. You listened to Connan McIver and frightened

yourself to death, and now you've listened to your uncle and engaged in guilty secrets . . . Did you go to the mill this afternoon?"

I nodded, too tired to speak.

"I see. I'm disappointed that you could be so deceitful, but it's no matter. They're quite good, aren't they? This one of you is excellent, and . . . oh! . . . yes, I see. Sleep now, my dear. You'd better stay in bed until morning. I won't take chances with your health."

I had done something terrible, I knew, but I couldn't seem to make my brain focus enough to discover what it was.

A knock on the door disturbed me and I woke to find Amy coming in with a tray which she set on the ottoman before closing the curtains against the darkness outside. As I struggled to sit up, she switched on the bedside lamp and set the tray across my knees.

"Your grandmother says you're not to think of coming down tonight," she told me. "Someone will be up to see you later—after they've eaten."

The meal looked good and smelled appetising, but I wasn't hungry. The pills had left me with a heavy head and no clear memory of my flight from the mill and my return home.

When I had eaten as much as I could, I put the tray aside and went to have a brief shower to try to clear my brain. I had no intention of staying in bed, but thought it politic to stay in my room at least for a while, so I put on a flowing kaftan in orange swirls, over a white polo-neck sweater, and sat before the mirror to brush out my long hair.

Haunted—that was how I looked; hollow-eyed and ill, with my naturally golden skin gone sallow. Perhaps Evan had been right and the accident had affected my mental balance. Perhaps grandmother was right when she insisted that I should rest more. But I could not. The feeling of Kismet was stronger, making me jumpy and fretful, and as I stared into the mirror I seemed to see a face form in the air behind me, a face carved of stone, leering obscenely.

I whirled round, but there was nothing there, only the

soft lamplight making misty shadows in the corners of the room—only the fear that beat insistently in my blood.

My hand twitched and something fluttered from the dressing table to the floor. It was the pamphlet about the church. Grandmother must have found it in my pocket with the photographs. And . . . Oh, God, had poor uncle Walter suffered for my lack of discretion? There had been pictures of Connan and Tom among the set.

Tom. Tom was coming at eight. It was now seven thirty. I had to be in the study to see him, for he made the darkness go away.

To pass the time, I opened the leaflet, scanning the lines of print without really reading anything. There was the church's history, dates, nothing of any significance, not hidden away here on the edge of Exmoor. Then a name leapt out at me—the name of Falconer.

'During the witch-hunts instigated by Cromwell,' I read, 'Ricard Falconer of Falconsgarth was accused of evil practices and hung within sight of his house. His family gave the body secret burial to hide their shame, but it is said that his daughter attempted to carve his name in the church, near the altar. She was discovered there and in the ensuing struggle was struck over the head and died. To this day there are marks on the church wall which may be an ill-defined R and F.'

The opening of the door startled me so much that I dropped the leaflet as I turned to see Peter coming in.

"Hello!" he said with a smile. "Aren't you supposed to be in bed?"

"I'm quite well," I said. "Really I am."

He strolled across the room, elegant in a lambswool sweater and sharp-creased slacks, and bent to pick up the pamphlet for me. As he did so, a dog howled outside, low and mournful, and I leapt to my feet to stare at the curtained window.

"I thought you said you were feeling better," Peter commented, straightening. "You're as nervous as a kitten. Look, Romaine, I do understand how you feel about that wood, but it's only a superstition. This time tomorrow we'll laugh about it."

I shivered, feeling cold although the room was over-warm, and the dog howled again, far away, threatening doom.

"It's only a dog," Peter said with a laugh. "Maybe it's old Maidie come to haunt us."

How could he be so callous? I wondered, saying flatly, "That isn't funny."

"No, you're right. Sorry. It's a shame about the dog."

"A shame?" I moved away from him, my arms curling round my body. "Are there rats in The Wood, Peter? Are there? So far from food? What do they live on?"

"You are in a peculiar mood," he said. "Grandmother's right—you'll have to relax more or you'll have a breakdown."

"You haven't answered my question," I said levelly. "Are there rats in that wood?"

A spasm of anger briefly crossed his handsome face. "No, not any more. Because I got rid of them! I'm sick of being cross-examined about that."

All at once I knew that he was lying and that Tom and Connan had been right. My cousin had deliberately laid poison in the hopes of killing the old man's dog. The realisation made me feel physically ill.

Perhaps something of what I was thinking showed on my face, for Peter sighed and reached out a hand to touch my shoulder. "Oh, come on, love. Let's not quarrel about . . ."

"Don't touch me!" I snapped, wrenching away, hating the thought of his hands on me. "And don't call me love!"

His smile was infinitely sad. "But that's what you are, Romaine. I can't help the way I feel. I love you. I want to marry you."

Thinking that this must be some horrible nightmare, I stared at him in silence. There was absolutely no emotion in his voice and I was tempted to ask him to repeat that astonishing announcement.

"Marry you?" I got out. "Peter . . . No. I'm sorry, but . . ."

"You don't love me?" he asked softly. "But you will, in time."

I tried to swallow the bramble that had got into my throat. "Love you? I don't even like you!"

He recoiled as if I had slapped him, his lips curling in an angry snarl. "Well, thank you! If that's the way you feel . . . Forget I mentioned it. Good night."

"Peter . . ." I said in a low voice as he reached the door. He stopped, glaring at me. "Well?"

"About those roses. Did you really order them for me?"

His mouth began to frame the word 'yes', then he hesitated and stared narrowly at me. "Why do you ask? Have you seen Tom Jamieson?"

"I believe I asked a question first," I replied, trembling. "Though I suppose you've answered it. They were Tom's roses, weren't they?"

"Yes, they were." Each word dripped bitterness. "And do you know why we didn't tell you?—Because there was a nasty little note with them and we didn't want to upset you. I don't suppose he mentioned that, did he? And while we're on the subject when did he get close enough to kiss you? That's what he said—'compensation for one measly kiss.' He signed it 'Halliday's cowman.' For a man you claim hardly to know, he seems to share some private jokes with you. But then you're not very fussy, are you, Romaine? You'd let anyone kiss you. You're a slut!"

With that final insult he slammed the door behind him and I sank down onto the edge of the bed, gathering fistfuls of coverlet. I didn't believe his excuses. Why had they even opened the florist's box? Why had they read the private note, which Tom had said was in a sealed envelope?

'They', I thought, were Peter—and grandmother. Peter had been out when the flowers came and it had been grandmother who told me they were a gift from him. Afterwards she had left the lunch table to speak to Peter before he saw me. So the whole thing had been her idea.

What was so terribly wrong with Tom Jamieson? His

illegitimacy? Or his closeness to Connan McIver? Both, probably. For the first time I was made fully aware of the hatred between the two families, and I knew that it was most virulent on the Faulkners' part. They detested Connan McIver and everyone he was close to. Why? Oh, why, why, why?

Closing my eyes tightly, determined not to give way to tears, I suddenly remembered that Tom was coming at eight o'clock. I was late already. It was ten past.

I flew on slippered feet along the hall and down the stairs, to the passage which led to the library, not caring if anyone saw me. The library was in darkness, heavy leather furniture lurking like sombre monsters, but I hurried across its carpet and wrenched open the study door.

My uncle was writing in one of the albums, but looked up blearily, surveying me through curling wreaths of cigar smoke.

"You're too late," he said listlessly. "He's been and gone. I told him you were ill."

My spirits drooped with an almost audible thud and I closed the door, leaning on it defeatedly. "What did he say?"

"Not much. I told him there was no point in his seeing you any more. There isn't any point, Romaine. For both of your sakes you're better apart, before it gets too serious. Take it from one who knows the dangers. I'm sorry, girl."

I reached blindly for a chair and sat down, feeling empty. "It wasn't your decision to make, uncle Walter. I'm a grown woman. If I want to see Tom . . ."

"Yes, I know," he sighed. "You won't listen to advice, any more than I did. But it's no good. It would never be allowed to come to anything. Don't you understand that?"

"Allowed?" I repeated miserably. "By whom?"

He dipped his pen into the white ink and bent once more over the book, shaking his unkempt grey head. It seemed that he did not intend to answer me, though I knew what he meant: the family would not allow it.

The pen worked delicately, with a slow, wristy motion, forming italics. I stood up and leaned on the desk, seeing that he had affixed one of the photographs of me, with the woods in the background. Not the one with the ivy. Beneath it he was writing, 'Romaine Faulkner, William's daughter.'

"Was she very angry about the photos?" I asked in a hushed voice.

Adding a full stop, he laid down his pen and tiredly lifted his head. "It wasn't your fault."

"But it was! I should have thought . . . What did she say?"

"Nothing much."

"She really doesn't mind your seeing Dick and Jill, you know," I told him. "And what can she do, anyway? All you have to do is stop worrying what she thinks."

His mouth stretched in a bitter smile. "I know that. But I do worry. 'What can she do?' She doesn't do anything. A few words, and a look. She can murder you with a look. Lydia can, too. Lydia should have been mother's daughter. They're two of a kind."

"They're totally different!" I argued. "Aunt Lydia's a dragon, but grandmother . . . grandmother's kind. She worries about everyone too much."

There was in his eyes a kind of rueful tenderness. "You should never have come here, Romaine," he said, and began to blow on the page to dry the ink.

"Well, I *am* here. And before I leave I'm going to make a few changes. This idiotic feud with Mr. McIver . . . Where are the other photographs? May I have the one of Tom?"

Keeping his eye on the page before him, he lifted a hand to point at the waste-bin in the corner. It was overflowing with papers and among them, torn into pieces, were the pictures of Tom and Connan.

I knelt by the bin, swallowing a ball of tears as I retrieved the pieces and tried to fit them together on the floor. There was no doubt in my mind who had done this. It had to be grandmother, destroying the photographs because she hated the two men they portrayed.

"Why did she do this?" I asked brokenly. "Why? Oh, uncle Walter, what is it all about? How can I fight it unless I know . . . "

"You can't fight it, my dear." He hesitated, looking un-happy, then suddenly left his seat and knelt beside me, fingers urgent on my wrist. "Romaine, go away from here. Go away soon, back to France, and forget you ever knew Falconsgarth. There's nothing here for you."

"Being away didn't help my father, did it?" I said in a low voice. "Tomorrow they cut The Wood. Will any of us be safe then, wherever we are?"

His eyes darted about my face and I could see his inner struggle—to agree with me, or to say, as the others said, that it was all superstitious nonsense.

"You don't know, either, do you?" I said. "You're not sure, either way. Can't you stop it, uncle Walter? Talk to grandmother. Make her see . . ."

"I?" He gave a choked laugh. "It's too late for that, Romaine. What will be, will be. Fate. Destiny. I've stopped caring what happens."

"But you don't . . ."

We both looked round, startled, as something tapped sharply on the window.

"Tom!" I started to rise, but my uncle's hand pinned me where I was.

"It might not be Tom. Stay here."

I watched him tread through the litter on the floor. He ducked behind the curtains and I heard the catch lift, then Tom's voice saying, "I know what you said, Mr. Faulkner, but I want to hear it from Romaine. Which is her room?"

I flung myself towards him, clawing back the curtains. "Tom!"

In the light from the window his eyes widened as he glanced angrily at my uncle. "You told me she was ill!"

"So I was," I said, leaning towards him as my uncle sighed and moved away. "Not ill, exactly, but . . . I'm glad you came back."

"I was going to throw stones at the window," he said with a wry grin. "And maybe climb the ivy. Like the prince in Rapunzel—you know?"

" I know." I smiled at him, relieved that he was there. " My hair isn't that long, though."

Behind me, uncle Walter sighed again, muttering about the open window.

" Can't you come out?" Tom asked.

" Not really. I'm supposed to be resting, but ... I'll meet you at the back door, for a few minutes. Don't go away."

" You're joking!" he said drily.

" You're mad," my uncle told me as I hurried for the door. " No good will come of it, Romaine."

" Something good has already happened!" I replied. " I feel alive again. See you later."

The ache in my side warned me to slow down as I left the library, so it was perhaps a minute before I turned the key in the back door and let myself into the night. Heavy clouds had prevented a frost but the darkness had an opaque quality that spoke of fog and smelled damp with rotting leaves. The light from the half-open doorway slanted across wisps of mist, showing me Tom's tall figure approaching. Three feet away, he hesitated, smiling at me uncertainly.

" This feels all wrong," he said quietly. " What are we doing sneaking about like a pair of criminals? Is it true, what Walter told me—you really think it's best that we shouldn't meet?"

" That's what *he* thinks," I replied, feeling the cold beginning to seep through my clothes and thin slippers. " I don't know what's best, yet. Do you?"

He shook his head, looking down at the path beneath his feet. " All I know is I want to find out whether there's any point to it or not. I keep telling myself you're out of reach, but ... "

" Why am I? Tom, that's not true!"

Smiling crookedly, he considered the short distance between us. " Not physically, it's not. But dare you outface your family openly? I'm not much good at this hole-and-corner stuff. I want to call for you, at the front door. That's how it should be."

"Then do it. Tomorrow night . . ." I stopped myself, remembering what the next day held in store. "They're coming to make a start on felling The Wood tomorrow," I added in a low voice.

"Yes," I know. You're not worried about that, are you?"

"Oh, please! Don't *you* tell me it's only a legend, too. I wish I could believe it, but I'm frightened, Tom."

In one swift movement he shrugged out of his jacket and stepped close to me, laying the garment round my shoulders, and suddenly I was in his arms, our mouths meeting as if from long practice. We kissed feverishly and clung together breathing as if exhausted.

"Don't be afraid," he said raggedly. "Nothing will happen to you. I won't let it."

"Oh, Tom." A laugh shivered out of me. "Will you take your shining sword and slay the demon for me? For a Faulkner?"

"You're not a Faulkner. You're a wild gypsy, and probably a witch."

"And you disliked me the moment you saw me."

I felt the amusement in him as his lips brushed my temple. "Is that the impression I gave? If I had disliked you, it would have been easier to be polite . . . You're still shivering."

"My feet are frozen."

His lips sought mine again, softly this time. "Even your lips are cold," he murmured against my skin.

"Yours aren't." I burrowed against him. "You're lovely and warm."

"You're lovely, too—and cold. You'd better go in. Tomorrow I'll . . ." He broke off, glancing up as the shaft of light from the door widened. When I looked round, Peter was standing on the doorstep, his face a mask of icy fury. The sight of him made Tom and me break apart.

"Tomorrow you'll what, Jamieson?" Peter asked in a soft, menacing voice.

"Tomorrow," Tom said levelly, "I shall call for Romaine at seven and take her out to dinner."

"No, Jamieson, you won't. My cousin doesn't want to see you again."

I was astounded. "Peter! This is the twentieth century! I don't need your permission to . . ."

"While you're under our roof you'll behave with a little decorum!" he interrupted fiercely. "We can't have every lout in the village knocking on the door."

Sensing the anger in Tom, I put out a hand to prevent him from rushing at my cousin. "That's grossly unfair, Peter."

"It's typical!" Tom snarled. "They'll probably lock you in your room, if they don't feed you rat-poison for defying them!"

I didn't really see what happened. In a whirl of motion Peter brushed past me and I heard the sickening thud of a fist against flesh. The next moment Tom was sprawled on the damp lawn, scrambling up with murderous rage making of his face a stranger's. I must have screamed his name, for I heard the echo ring mockingly through the woods before being swallowed in the mist, and as he hesitated grandmother's voice said from behind me, "Don't brawl, Peter. It's so undignified. Good evening, Mr. Jamieson. Do you make it a practice to call secretly at back doors?"

"It wasn't his fault!" I protested.

She turned a mild face towards me. "Then was it yours? I'm surprised at you, Romaine. Were you brought up to be underhand and deceitful? Is this the thanks we get for giving you shelter? I have no intention of discussing it out here. It's cold, and there's a draught blowing right through the house from this door. Considering that you were ill enough to need putting to bed only a few hours ago, it's rather inconsiderate of Mr. Jamieson to keep you out here in weather like this. Why don't you invite him in?"

Helpless, I glanced at Tom, who shook his head vigorously and reached to take his jacket from my shoulders. "Your grandmother's right," he said. "Good night, Romaine."

"I'll see you tomorrow?" I asked anxiously.

His eyes were unhappy, blood trickling from his lip. He

glanced bleakly at grandmother. " No, I don't think so. I'll keep to my place from now on. Good night."

Feeling as though I had been betrayed, I watched him stride away until he was lost in the darkness; then a gentle hand came on my arm and I saw grandmother's face filled with concern.

" I did try to warn you, my dear," she said softly. " Come, let's go inside and get warm."

In the red sitting room I sat by the fire, my head in my hands. For a short while I had believed that I could fight the forces which were gathering against me, but Tom's defection had destroyed that hope. Uncle Walter had been right—I should leave Falconsgarth and go back where I belonged, far away from the darkness that loomed over this corner of Devon.

" I'm sorry you had to learn the hard way," grandmother said as Peter came in still flexing his hand as if it hurt. " A man like that . . . You were a challenge to him, that's all. It would have been no fun for him to call normally. There was more excitement in clandestine meetings. You heard what he said when I invited him in."

" You knew he wouldn't come," I said dully.

" I gave him the choice. He chose to retreat. Don't blame me for his lack of moral fibre. I do understand how you feel, my dear, but it was as well for you to see him in his true colours before you became too deeply embroiled. Now I suggest you go to bed before you drop. I'll send Amy up with some hot chocolate. You'll have this unfortunate episode in proportion by tomorrow."

Too despondent to argue, I heaved myself out of the chair and trailed across the hearth rug to drop a kiss on her forehead. Only as I straightened did I notice the empty space on the mahogany table, where the vase of roses had stood.

" I threw them out," grandmother said. " They were withered, and dropping petals everywhere."

I stared at the table, slow to comprehend. The roses had been fine that morning when I changed their water. They had been velvety and beautiful, but they had been sent by Tom, and now she knew that I was aware of it; so she had thrown them away.

"They never last long," she said. "Hot-house blooms."

"Yes," I said dazedly, and went to bed to weep helplessly into my pillow.

After a terrible, endless night when I was by turns hot and cold, wakeful and dreaming, I roused myself early and sat watching dawn come over The Wood. There was no spectacular sunrise, only a gradual lightening of the clouds until they were a sullen grey. The woods below were still wreathed in mist that clung among the trees, and the distance was veiled by fog. It was going to be a damp, still, awful day.

Unable to face the thought of breakfast with the family, I had a bath and dressed warmly in slacks and thick sweater, because I intended to be out on the hill when the men came. I had to be there to witness whatever might happen. But I almost delayed too long. As I was leaving my room I saw a tractor grinding up the hill, dragging a trailer on which two men were sitting, and in the trailer were machines which looked like electric saws.

Clambering through the dead branches and leaves in the lower woods, I gained the slope beyond just as the first saw started its clamour on the still air, buzzing like a furious bee. I walked as fast as I could, up the uneven hillside. The men were at the far side of The Wood, two of them sizing up the trees while the third was hidden with the saw. And I also saw Connan McIver striding up the hill with the help of his stick, hood thrown back and his face grim.

Unable to think of anything to do, I stood and watched what would happen.

"You men!" Connan's deep voice boomed out, and the two I could see turned to him. "Do you know what you're doing? This place is cursed. Don't you know what happened the last time those trees were touched?"

The men glanced at each other, eyebrows raised, and one of them twirled his finger beside his head, in the sign for madness.

I must have moved closer, for I now saw that the third man was lopping branches off the dead half of the split tree.

"A man was killed!" Connan declaimed as the saw fell briefly silent. "A bolt of lightning struck him down. You can see what it did to the tree. Ask in the village, if you doubt me. Ask them what happened to Ned Freeman. Or ask his brother Ben, who was here when it happened."

"What's he on about?" the man in the wood called.

"Something about a curse," the chuckle went back.

The third man laid the saw aside, clambering out among the shrubs and branches until he reached the fence. "Ned Freeman?" he asked of Connan, his face pale beneath a red knitted hat. "Did ye say Ned Freeman?"

"I did," the old man replied.

To my amazement, the man crossed himself swiftly. "Is this the place? I'd heard about it, but I didn't know it was this place."

"Devil's Wood," Connan intoned in a voice so heavy with doom that the tiny hairs on the back of my neck stood to attention, sending shivers along my spine. "This place is unsanctified ground and a curse is on it. Ned Freeman died here."

"And my father died in France, at the same time," I added, unable to prevent myself.

The workmen turned in surprise at finding me there, though the man in the red hat did not seem half amused, unlike his friends.

"The curse is on the Faulkners," I told them. "If The Wood falls, so will the family. Six years ago one tree was marked. There—you can see it. The man who did it died, and so did my father, a Faulkner."

"But it was Lady Faulkner who ordered this done!" one of them protested.

"Lady Faulkner chooses to thumb her nose at Fate," Connan replied. "Last time her son died, and Ned Freeman died. Who will it be this time? You? Or you?"

I had not noticed Peter coming up behind me until he said

angrily, panting from the hasty climb, "That's enough of that, McIver. This copse is coming down. You men get on with it if you value your jobs. Mr. Fenniston wouldn't be very pleased if you stopped work because of the ravings of a crazy old man."

"Yer sister agrees with him," the man in the red hat said.

Peter flung me a glance of pure fury. "She's not my sister, she's my cousin, and she's been ill. She imagines things. Get on with it, or by Heaven I'll get Fenniston here to sort you out! As for you, McIver—stay out of this. I'm just about sick of your interference."

The two sceptics shrugged and turned back to their work, but the red-hatted one hesitated for a moment, then climbed over the fence, removing his gloves.

"I value my job, but I value my life more. I knew Ned Freeman when we were lads."

"Oh, come on, Stan," one of his workmates said scornfully. "You don't believe in old wives' tales, do you? We need three men for this job."

"Then get someone else!" was the reply. He glanced at Peter, then at me. "May I be forgiven if I've caused any harm, miss. I'm a God-fearing man, but there's things God has no say in. That I know. Good day to you."

As the man walked hurriedly away, half-sliding down the hill towards the McIvers' cottage, I heard Peter swearing angrily under his breath. The other men were looking at him as if waiting for orders.

Eventually he swung round, flinging his arms out. "Well, get on with it! It doesn't take three men to cut down a few trees, does it? I'll phone Mr. Fenniston and have him send someone else, but meantime there must be something you can be doing.

"Romaine, get back to the house. You've no business out here. If you're not back in five minutes I'll come and fetch you —by force, if necessary!"

There was silence as he strode away, making towards Falconsgarth. I was aware of the two workmen watching me in a puzzled fashion, but I turned defeatedly to Connan McIver.

"It's no good, is it? Now we find out how true the legend is. Thank you for trying."

He beckoned me over to him and surreptitiously handed me an envelope. "From Tom. I know how things are. Heaven protect you, lass—if there is such a place."

Hopelessly, I watched as he, too, walked away from The Wood; then I put the letter in my pocket and began to trudge towards Falconsgarth.

In my room, I read the letter from Tom.

'My dear Romaine, I saw in your face what you thought of me, but it wasn't cowardice, only bowing to the inevitable. I've lived with Faulkner spite for too long to risk bringing it on you. Your uncle knew best, after all, though God knows I wish things had been different. There's so much I want to say, but it looks corny written down. Maybe it's best not to say it at all. Take care of yourself. My love, Tom.'

I lay face down on the bed, the letter clutched beneath me, and let the slow tears fall. With the sound of the electric saw as a distant lullaby, I fell into a dreamless sleep.

Surprisingly, I woke refreshed, without a trace of the headache that had niggled at me for days. There was no sign of the men at The Wood and when I glanced at my watch I saw that it was lunchtime. They were probably in the pub.

"Feeling better?" grandmother asked brightly as I went into the dining room. "We thought we'd let you sleep, since you seem to need the rest. You don't mind our starting?"

"Not at all." I sank into my usual place beside Peter. "Where's uncle Walter?"

"He's late, too," my aunt growled. "But he possesses a watch and he knows we lunch at one. He's probably asleep over those wretched albums."

"Anyway," Peter said, carving me a slice of cold beef, "the work is well under way at The Wood. That dead tree is entirely down, and there haven't been any celestial bolts of lightning. So now what do you say Romaine?"

"Leave her alone, Peter," grandmother put in. "Romaine isn't the first to have believed that legend. Have some potato, my dear, and help yourself to salad. Peter, when you've done that go and fetch your father, will you? If people are absent from meals it makes things very inconvenient for Amy."

Stifling a sigh of annoyance, Peter put down the carvers and left the room.

I found myself picking at my food, concerned about uncle Walter. Usually he was punctual to the minute to avoid 'making waves' as he called it. It was puzzling, but I would be lying if I said I was expecting what happened.

All at once Peter was standing in the doorway, looking grim. "Mother . . . I think you'd better come. He's been drinking and I can't rouse him."

"The fool!" aunt Lydia hissed. "Excuse me, please."

When they had gone, there was a moment's silence before grandmother said quietly, "Your uncle has a problem, Romaine. Perhaps you've noticed he never touches alcohol."

"I know. He told me. Excuse me, grandmother." Something made me want to be there, not to leave my uncle to the mercies of his wife and son.

I reached the study in time to see aunt Lydia shaking her husband violently by the shoulder as he lay across the desk. A bottle of whisky stood by his right hand, only the dregs remaining in it.

"Walter!" my aunt screamed in his ear. "Walter, wake up, you fool!"

He slid from her hands and quietly folded to the floor, as unobtrusively as he might have done if he had been alive.

SEVEN

It was very quiet in the house, but it was not peaceful. Underneath the silence there was screaming—at least, that was how it felt to me. Perhaps the screams were my own, unvoiced but raging against the insanity of death, the futility of defying the forces of evil.

The doctor had been, and the police. They took away an empty bottle of sleeping tablets and they took uncle Walter. The four of us gathered in the red sitting room, temporarily drifting. Grandmother was quiet but outwardly controlled; my aunt sat like a frozen carcass, hands clutched in her lap kneading themselves; Peter paced the room, constantly looking out of the window; and I felt helpless—and angry, too.

"You must order those men to leave The Wood," I said into the silence, my voice trembling with the effort of keeping it low when I wanted to shout. "You must, grandmother!"

"Oh, for God's sake!" Peter exclaimed. "Don't you understand? He killed himself. It wasn't anything to do with the legend. He committed the last spineless act of a spineless life!"

My aunt thrust her fist against her mouth in anguish. "Peter!"

"Well, it's true! He hasn't suddenly become a paragon just because he's dead."

"That's quite enough," grandmother put in quietly. "He was your father, Peter, and he was my son. We'll show a little respect, if you please."

"You mean we'll make ourselves hypocrites!" he returned,

D

but she gave him a flashing look that silenced him and he turned again to the window, tapping his fingers against the sill.

None of them cared, I thought in sad amazement. Not one of them really cared that they had made uncle Walter unhappy enough to take his own life. Though of course they wouldn't see it that way. None of them would accept any blame.

" And where are you going?" Peter demanded as I started for the door.

I paused, deliberately waiting for a moment before I looked over my shoulder at him and said levelly, " I'm going to the church, to pray—if you have no objections."

He jerked his head and turned away, restless hands clasped behind his back.

What made me go to the church I don't know, for when I got there I found there were no words to express what I felt, so I sent up a wordless plea and stopped to run my fingers over the cold, blank marble on the bottom of the slab where my father and grandfather were commemorated. Soon uncle Walter's name would join theirs.

And still the men were working at The Wood—I had heard the saw as I left the house. Grandmother was still ignoring the curse, though now she had lost both of her sons.

In the gloom and silence of the church, Evan's voice repeated in my head, " The Devil can only work through men's minds." Was that what had happened? Had an evil force possessed my uncle to take those pills and then drink himself into oblivion, because of The Wood? Dear God, help me! Make me believe it isn't true!

The misty November day was waning as I left the church and walked back through the village, comfortless. There was no help for me. No help anywhere.

But even as the thought came, a blue car slid to a halt beside me, the nearside door opening as the vehicle stopped, and there was Tom, leaning across the passenger seat to look at me, both shame-faced and hopeful.

" Want a lift?"

Nodding, I climbed into the car and closed the door, staring through the windscreen.

"Aren't you talking to me?" Tom asked.

I turned to look at his strong, attractive face, the dark hair dishevelled, grey eyes pleading. " It's not that, Tom. It's just . . . my uncle died today."

There was a moment's stunned silence as he stared at me incredulously. "Walter?" he breathed eventually. "How?"

"He seems to have committed suicide—with whisky and pills. They're doing a post-mortem. It's not real to me yet. I've just been to the church. I had to get out of the house. They don't care, you see. None of them."

"Oh, love!" He reached for me and I found myself weeping against his shoulder, grateful for the comfort of his arms.

He took me back to Falconsgarth, all the way to the door, then insisted on coming in with me despite my protests. We were met in the hall by Peter, who had apparently seen us arrive for he was already bridling.

"Jamieson . . ."

Tom's arm tightened around me, but his voice was even. " I found Romaine in the village. She was upset, so I gave her a lift. I wanted to say . . . I'm sorry about your father. And if you can find something wrong with that then I'm sorry for you, too."

"Mr. Jamieson . . ." grandmother said from the sitting room doorway. " It was kind of you. Thank you."

"Mr. Faulkner was always kind to me," Tom told her. " I shall miss him. Goodbye, Romaine."

Numbed, I watched him open the door. "Goodbye, Tom."

"I mean—for now," he said, and gave me a small, encouraging smile.

The family said no more about my meeting with Tom, but Peter kept sending me dark glances and I knew he was still angry.

That evening I went to find him, to try to amend the wrong I had done. He was in the television room, where the colour set was showing some comedy programme which jarred on my nerves in a house of mourning.

"Peter . . ."

He leapt up from his chair and turned the television off with a snapping motion, whirling to glare at me aggressively. "Well? What is it now?"

"I came to say, I'm sorry—for what I said last night. I could have been kinder. I didn't mean to hurt you."

"Oh, forget it," he said irritably, throwing himself back into the chair. "If I had known Jamieson had got there before me . . ."

"It isn't like that!" I protested. "It has nothing to do with Tom. I just don't . . . feel that way about you."

"You made that painfully obvious. Oh, go away, Romaine. Can't you see I'd rather be alone? Go and meet your country bumpkin. I couldn't care less."

Although my temper rose in Tom's defence, I made no reply. It was pointless to argue with him. I could only hope that in time he would forgive me and at least make an attempt to be friendly.

In time? How long did I intend to stay at Falconsgarth? The doctors had said I should convalesce for at least a month before trying to return to work, though I had written to my publisher employers to tell them to fill my post if they wished. There would be a great deal for me to do when I went back to France. The lawyers were at present sorting out legalities, but I would need to be there to supervise the final disposition of mother's belongings.

And where did that leave Tom? Falling in love with him would be an extra complication. I could not see myself settling down in Winterford, on the doorstep of Falconsgarth, not when Tom felt about my family as he did. The seeds of discord were already sown, before our relationship had properly begun. But the thought of going away, never to see Tom again, was even worse. I hardly knew him, I rationalised. It would be easy to break ties that were not firmly bound. If I were sensible I would gently hold him off, to prevent either of us being hurt. But it seemed that love and common sense had little connection, for I knew that as long as I remained at Falconsgarth I would want to see Tom Jamieson at every opportunity, without giving a fig for the long-term consequences.

The following day was an eternity of greyness, rain cascading down the windows, making a sound like sighing on the ivy leaves. The men did not return to the hilltop and it was not the weather to go out, though Peter was absent for most of the day making arrangements. I gathered that grandmother had ascertained that uncle Walter had not left a Will at the office of the family lawyer. After all, I heard her say to aunt Lydia, Walter had very little to leave. Peter must have his personal possessions and my aunt would keep what little money there was.

Feeling restless, I ventured into the study and found Amy there surveying the chaos.

"This place ought to be tidied up," she said. "I was never allowed to touch it before. I'm afraid of tampering with private things, that's the trouble. Mrs. Faulkner says I can clear the lot out, as far as she's concerned, but ... Well, I don't know. It seems a shame when these things meant so much to Mr. Faulkner. And there may be things Mr. Peter will want to keep. It's a big job."

"Would you like me to make a start?" I asked. "Yes, really, I'd be glad of something to do. If I sort everything out, then Peter can look through it when he has time. There's no rush, is there?"

She seemed glad to be relieved of the responsibility and, as I knew, she had plenty of other work to occupy her. A woman came in to do heavy jobs and laundry twice a week and my aunt helped out—with light chores like cleaning the silver— but otherwise Amy ran the huge house single-handed.

Although it did not worry me to be in the study, I soon began to understand what Amy had meant about tampering with private things. This had been my uncle's one small area of privacy, and presumably even the piles of old magazines had been precious to him. There were magazines on photography, philately, and a few girly books. Feeling sad for the empty life he had been forced to lead these past few years, I sorted the books and put them in neat piles on the floor.

There was an empty cardboard box behind the chair and I used it as a trash-box, emptying the litter bin—the shreds of photographs could not be pieced together—and the two overflowing ashtrays, plus everything else which I was sure was rubbish. Only then did I turn to the desk, which was exactly as my uncle had left it, even to the whisky bottle which stood like a defiant reminder of five years of abstinence and misery.

The photograph albums were all on the desk. Wondering if he had brought them right up to date before he died, I opened the top one, the latest one, finding each photograph neatly marked as always up to the final one of myself. I idly turned the page, wondering who, if anyone, would keep the albums now, and found the photograph of my uncle which I had taken only the previous Saturday. He stared up at me solemnly, causing a curious little quirk of my heart. Beneath it, he had written in a shaking hand unlike his usual careful copper-plate, 'Walter Frederick Faulkner, died 14th November' and the year.

Near the spine of the book there was a slender key, which I picked up and turned thoughtfully in my hand.

He had prepared very carefully, I thought, sinking down into his chair as a weary depression closed round me. All at once I saw significance in several things he had said to me—'Just once before I die, I want someone unbiased to hear my side of it,' and, 'I do want to see those pictures, Romaine. Tomorrow they start felling The Wood.' He had planned his death, I was sure, to coincide with the cutting of the trees. It was not the act of a moment's despair but a deliberate operation carried out calmly and coldly. 'What will be, will be,' he had said. 'Fate. Destiny. I've stopped caring.'

Choked with tears, I went to give aunt Lydia the key I had found.

"I don't particularly want it," she said. "I expect it fits the drawer of the desk. There's nothing else he kept locked. Whatever sordid little secrets he kept in there, I'm not interested. I suggest you burn whatever there is—and burn those horrible obscene magazines, too. I let him have his little perversions, but I would prefer not to have them polluting the house any longer."

Returning to the study, I flicked through the 'obscene' magazines and found them pretty innocuous; I had seen worse pictures on the front covers of books on public display. 'I should never have married Lydia,' my uncle had said.

Sitting back on my heels, I wondered why only now, when it was too late, did I see significance in seemingly throw-away remarks. There were so many things I had wanted to ask him —about my father particularly—that now I would never know. If I had really been gifted with foresight I would have known what he was planning, but instead I had thought the warnings were for me.

The key was still in my hand. I moved back to the desk and tried it in the lock of the top drawer, where it fitted snugly. But I didn't turn it because suddenly this was too much like prying. Someone else could have the task of clearing the drawer.

"God, it stinks in here!" Peter commented sourly, bursting in so suddenly that he startled me. "I don't know how you can stand it. Why don't you open a window?"

"Because it's raining, in case you hadn't noticed."

"Oh, I noticed. I've been out in it. They've arranged an inquest for tomorrow, though it's a foregone conclusion. The funeral will be on Friday afternoon. Oh, and your boyfriend's on the phone. You can take it on the extension in the library." And he was gone as abruptly as he had come.

I hurried through into the next room, where the shelves of books stood silent, impressive but largely unread.

"Hello? Tom?"

"Oh, hello, Romaine. I was beginning to think they'd forgotten about me. How are you today?"

I sat down on the big, shining desk, looking out of the window at the sodden woods as a tiny spurt of joy lightened my spirits. " I'm fine, thank you. How are you?"

" Lonely," was his answer. " I'm glad to hear you're sounding a bit more cheerful. You looked like a ghost yesterday. I hate to admit that I've been worrying about a Faulkner, but . . ."

"Can you cut this chit-chat short?" Peter's voice broke in. " I need to make some important calls and I can't do that while you two are discussing your health." There was a click as he put down his extension.

I heard Tom swear to himself. " When am I going to be able to talk to you without your family getting in the way?" he asked bitterly. " I just called to say that I think it would be more tactful to play it cool until after your uncle's funeral. Do you know when that will be?"

" Friday," I said.

" I'll see you then. How do you feel about having dinner on Saturday? Is it too soon?"

" I'm not sure. Let me see how things go. I'll tell you on Friday."

" Beginning to get to you, are they? Maybe your uncle was right."

" That's what you said in your letter," I reminded him sadly.

" I know. My head keeps telling me I'm crazy, but the rest of me . . . Let's leave it until Friday. Maybe things will have calmed down by then. Did the roses arrive?"

I hesitated, deciding to tell a half-truth. " Yes. They're beautiful, Tom. Thank you."

" Did you read the note?"

Again it was a moment before I replied, " No," which was the truth, even though Peter had told me the gist.

" Curiosity killed the cat," Tom said misinterpreting my tone. " Anyway, you know I didn't mean it. Oh, by the way, Con said I was to tell you that something happened at The Wood yesterday. The men left in a hurry. They told him they wouldn't be back."

"Did they? I thought it was the weather that was keeping them away. Grandmother hasn't said anything about it."

"Well, that's what Con said, anyway. He and Mum send their love."

"That was nice of them. Give mine to them, and keep some for yourself."

This time it was Tom who hesitated. "I might keep all of it. Will you risk that?"

"What's to risk?" I said in a low voice. "*Au 'voir, mon coeur.*"

"*Je t'aime,*" said Tom, and broke the connection.

I stared at the receiver, hardly knowing whether to laugh or cry. I had called him 'my heart' thinking he wouldn't understand, but he must have done, for he had replied, 'I love you.'

"Well, put it down!" Peter's voice said faintly.

Furious, I slammed the receiver into the cradle, hoping it deafened him. How dare he listen in on a private conversation? How much had he heard? I began to understand why uncle Walter had grown so secretive. It seemed the only way of keeping anything to oneself.

The following morning the family all went to the inquest, after long discussions as to who should go and who should not. All three of them wanted to be there, for reasons I could only guess at; so I was left alone in the house with Amy.

I was in the study tidying the bookshelf when the housekeeper came to say that 'a deputation from the W.I.' had called to see Lady Faulkner, but in her absence they would like a word with me. Mystified, I made my way to the drawing room where four smartly-dressed women were seated uneasily on the blue and gold brocade, talking in whispers which stopped as I appeared.

Quite what they had expected I'm not sure, but it certainly wasn't a girl in jeans, with her hair flying loose and dust on her sweater. And when I said, "Good morning, ladies," my accent gave them further pause.

The leader of the deputation stood up. "Miss Faulkner?" she queried in disbelief.

"That's right. What can I do for you? I haven't been at Falconsgarth very long, as you probably know, but . . . I'm willing to listen. Please—sit down. I've asked the housekeeper to make coffee."

I seated myself by the fireplace, where the electric fire was glowing to add its warmth to the central heating. The leader sat down, on the edge of the settee, holding her gloves over her handbag, one hand adjusting the curls which peeped from beneath the brim of a large green hat.

"We do realise that this is not really the time to bother Lady Faulkner," she began, "but we were afraid that if the matter was left any longer . . . Oh, I'm sorry. I ought to introduce myself. I'm Mrs. Wells and these ladies are the members of the ' Save the Hall ' committee, from the Women's Institute."

Light began to glimmer through my puzzlement. "The hall? The one my grandfather gave you?"

"Exactly!" she sighed with relief. "You know about it, I see."

"No, not really. Are you collecting money for the fund?"

"No, Miss Faulkner, we are not. And if we were we would not apply to Falconsgarth for help. The fact is—we have heard that Lady Faulkner intends to sell our hall to some peculiar religious group. Our letters to her have gone unanswered. Yesterday there were men at the hall measuring up—complete strangers. We want to know exactly what the position is."

"I'm afraid I don't understand," I said. "If you were given the hall, how can my grandmother sell it?"

"That's exactly the point. We now discover that the deeds never changed hands. We have nothing in writing to prove our claim, though over the last thirty years we have paid for the upkeep of the place, had it rewired, and built a new kitchen. According to our solicitor, we have no redress, not officially, so unless we can appeal to Lady Faulkner's sense of fair play we shall lose our meeting place and there's no-where else in the village that will be suitable."

She was getting agitated as Amy came in with the trolley and there was a pause while everyone was served with coffee.

" It's just not fair! " one of the other women said. " That hall was built for us by Sir Gerald's father. His wife was President—founder President of our branch. *She* took a proper interest in the village."

The others glanced at her as if to silence the implied criticism of my grandmother, and Mrs. Wells appealed to me, " Will you please talk to Lady Faulkner? If she will give us time, we'll try to raise the money."

" We shouldn't have to," the oldest put in stubbornly. " Sir Gerald *gave* us that hall. I was there when the announcement was made. He said he'd gladly be rid of the trouble of collecting the little rent we paid—everybody laughed at that. And we clapped and cheered. It was a wonderful day. Now to have it sold from under us, without so much as a by-your-leave . . . It's a real slap in the face."

They all looked at me, waiting for my comment.

" I'm sure there must be some mistake," I said with more conviction than I felt. " Do you know for certain that the hall is to be sold?"

" Apparently," Mrs. Wells said, " one of our members spoke to these men who were measuring up and they told her they were negotiating to buy the hall. They said it would all be settled in a week or two, and the W.I. would have to move out. Miss Faulkner . . . I apologise for bringing this up at a time of grief for your family, but we really are desperate. People in the village are angry about it. Rumours have been flying for some time. Everybody understood that the hall belonged to the W.I. But if we have to, we'll buy it—if only Lady Faulkner will give us time."

" Leave it with me," I said, bewildered by the whole thing. " I'll find out the truth of the matter and let you know. Do you have a phone number?"

She wrote it on a page from a notepad and gave it to me.

" I'm from the next village, as you see. We have members from a wide area. If the hall goes, this branch of the W.I. will fold, and in its place you'll have these cranks ... I wouldn't have said all this to your grandmother, of course, not at a time like this. We're all very sorry about your . . ."

" My uncle," I supplied. " Thank you. Yes, my grandmother does have a lot on her mind at the moment, but I'll do what I can for you."

" You're your father's daughter," the oldest woman approved. " *He* wouldn't have stood by and let her get away with this. *He* was a real gentleman, not like the rest. It's no wonder he left in disgust, though if you ask me she was glad to see the back of him. Never did get on, those two."

" Didn't they?" I said in amazement.

Mrs. Wells stood up suddenly, the others all following her example. " We mustn't keep you. Thank you so much for giving us your time, Miss Faulkner. We'll see ourselves out. Good morning."

They filed past me, shaking hands, saying " Thank you," and " Goodbye ", until the oldest one confronted me, taking my hand in a steely grip, piercing eyes staring into mine.

" No, they didn't," she said. " And you be careful, my lovely. She won't like being crossed. She can be very nasty when she's crossed."

" Mrs. Lambert!" Mrs. Wells hissed, pulling her away, smiling brightly at me. " Thank you again, Miss Faulkner."

Bemused, I stood in the doorway and watched them leave. Poor Mrs. Lambert was being chafed at for saying too much, I could see, but I was grateful to her for giving me a little extra piece to add to the puzzle.

The inquest had, predictably, brought a verdict of suicide while of unsound mind. The family seemed annoyed that uncle Walter could have brought such disgrace on their name, and the general impression I gathered was that this was typical of a weak man who, in their opinion, had never been much use to anyone. It was a cruel epitaph from the people who had been closest to him. And, perhaps, I was not in the state of mind to be generous towards them. I suspect their feelings can not have been quite so cut and dried as I imagined.

Over lunch, I raised the question of the W.I. hall by innocently remarking that a deputation from the Women's Institute had called with condolences. It was obvious from the sharp glances directed towards me by three pairs of eyes that the family knew very well that there had been another reason for the committee's call. Quite suddenly, the Faulkners were on the defensive.

"They were also asking about their hall," I went on. "They've heard a rumour that you're selling it, grandmother, but that can't be true because the hall already belongs to them."

"That's a lie!" Peter growled. "They were allowed use of the hall, rent-free, in return for their contribution to the upkeep of the place. The deed is still in our possession."

"But one of the ladies clearly remembers the day when grandfather *gave* them the hall," I argued. "She says they cheered and . . ."

"Romaine," grandmother put in gently. "My dear, I was there, too, and indeed there was great jubilation—when your grandfather told them he was waiving the rent. He was a philanthropist, you know. But the hall is something of a white elephant to the estate, and we have had a very good offer for it. I have written to the W.I. to explain the position."

"Then your letter must have gone astray," I said. "The ladies were very upset. They ask for time—to raise the money themselves and . . ."

A harsh laugh from Peter interrupted me. "They couldn't raise that much if we gave them five years."

Perhaps I was becoming over-suspicious, but I didn't believe them. The committee would not have braved grandmother's wrath if they had not had a very strong case. They wished to appeal to her sense of 'fair-play', they had said, but it was becoming more and more apparent that the fragile old lady, delicate as a water-colour, had very few scruples when it came to 'playing' that kind of game.

By acknowledging my total ignorance of English business practices, I ascertained a few more salient facts about the deal over the hall, intending to see what I could do to delay the negotiations. Mrs. Lambert had said my father would not have stood by and let it happen, and I had a feeling that my grandfather would have felt the same, so I had no compunction about playing a little dirty myself.

In the library, I stood before the portrait of my grandfather, studying the almost-smile on his face.

" You're with me, aren't you?" I asked.

" Talking to spirits now?" Peter said cynically from the study doorway. " Where have you put the key to the drawer? Mother said you found it."

" So I did. If you look, it's in the lock."

Curiosity made me follow him into the study and I saw him open the drawer, rustling among the contents.

" Good God!" he said in disgust. " Look at these, Romaine. Stories. Good heavens, is that what he did with his time?"

He pulled out a sheaf of handwritten pages, riffling through them, and without bothering to read a word, he hurled them towards my trash box, so that they scattered everywhere, one or two actually hitting the target.

" So much for the great writer! He couldn't even have a dark secret worth finding out. Well, it's all yours. I don't want any of these things, except for the albums. They might fetch a few pounds one of these days. Oh, and keep your eye open for a big silver watch in a box. I want that. The rest you can throw out, and good riddance." With which he strode out, trampling all over his father's manuscripts.

My eyes went to the shelf which I had tidied only that morning. Between two books there stood the battered box which contained the turnip watch. It was as close as that, but Peter did not know it, which only showed the immense gap there had been between him and his father. It was sad; it was infuriating; it was unbearably painful that such things

could be true among people who were supposed to care about
one another.

I bent and began to gather the handwritten pages of uncle
Walter's stories, reading a few lines here and there. They
were not great literature, but possibly worth a read, if I could
get them back into the right order. I had to smile, rather
sadly, at my uncle's pen-name 'Falconer'. Poor uncle
Walter's most sacred private things were, after all, rather
pitiful. When I tried to open the drawer further, to retrieve
the rest of the manuscripts, it became stuck. I took a firm grip
of the handle and tugged sharply, so that the whole drawer
shot out and tipped over, its contents sliding to the floor. It
happened so suddenly that I dropped the drawer and found,
when I bent to rescue it, that a false bottom had come loose.
Beneath it there was a large book with blue cardboard covers.

A pulse in my throat beat uncomfortably hard as I picked
up the book, but before I looked at it something made me
check that the library was empty. I carefully closed the study
door and turned the key, with the feeling that uncle Walter
had led me to the book and wanted me to be the first to look
at it—perhaps the only one. He seemed very close to me at
that moment, his vague blue eyes and wan, tired smile just
out of sight behind the air in the room.

Carefully, almost reverently, I laid the blue book on the
desk, opening it at the first page.

It was just another album, I thought, deriding myself for
imagining deep mysteries. There were pictures of a young girl
with fair hair done in long plaits. She wore various costumes
of baggy slacks and long, full skirts, and further on her braids
were wound round her head, making her look older. Then she
had a baby in her arms, and later a toddler clutching her
hand. There, to my surprise, was a young uncle Walter with
the same dark-haired child and the girl with her arm through
his. Behind them a beach was crowded with people.

I swallowed thickly, feeling sick with apprehension. Uncle
Walter had, indeed, kept a dark secret. The pictures were a
record of a sweetheart who, it appeared, had become wife

and then mother, but it wasn't aunt Lydia and the child was not Peter. I was horribly sure that I knew the identity of that fair-haired girl, but her name refused to surface in my mind.

The next page was blank. Uncle Walter had written across it in black ink, ' The years between ', and beyond it there were more pictures, in which the child had grown into a sturdy boy at various stages through youth and into young manhood, by which time there was no mistaking him.

It was Tom.

EIGHT

On the morning of uncle Walter's funeral there was an argument at the breakfast table because Mr. Fenniston had phoned to say that his men were unable to fulfil their contract at The Wood. Other commitments had arisen, more urgent. Lady Faulkner would have to hire someone else.

" You wouldn't believe it! " Peter fumed. " I'm beginning to think there *is* a jinx on that place. First Ned Freeman gets himself killed and now Fenniston ducks out with excuses— and they are excuses, grandmother. He was too vague to be telling the truth. If you ask me, it's McIver we have to thank for this. He probably went up there prophesying doom and destruction . . . And what are you smiling about, Romaine? I suppose you're pleased this happened. You actually believe The Wood killed my father. Well, it didn't. Barbiturates and whisky killed him."

I don't think I had been smiling, but I may have been looking relieved because, after all, he had not heard much of my telephone conversation with Tom. No, I most definitely was not smiling, not with the burden of the secret I now held in trust. With all my heart I wished I had not found that blue book with its tell-tale pictures of a forbidden love. 'History repeating itself,' uncle Walter had said when I came sneaking home with Tom, as my uncle must have sneaked off to meet Tom's mother. But I was sure that no one had bothered to tell Tom who his real father was, and if he found out . . . I dare not even think of the possibilities.

The blue album was now in my room, locked in my overnight bag, whose key was on a chain round my neck. The false bottom to the drawer lay underneath the pile of rubbish in a box in the cellar, waiting to be burned, and no one would ever know there had been a secret compartment. But my dilemma remained—had I any right to keep the truth a secret, and if not, then with whom did I share it first?

As for The Wood, I was relieved that the men were not coming back. There was still a pall of gloom over Falconsgarth, but it was the gloom of mourning. Of course it was. Devil's Wood had taken its vengeance already.

I tried to shut these pagan thoughts from my mind during the funeral service, but the feeling had come back strongly, as though it had given me brief respite to grieve over my uncle and was now taking hold again. Grandmother held tightly to my arm as we followed aunt Lydia and Peter behind the coffin into church, which was almost full of people. I saw Connan McIver and Ruth, and Tom, and bent comfortingly towards grandmother to hide my own tears.

Evan spoke briefly about a fine man who had had many friends and of the sorrow of the ending of that life under the influence of sickness. He apparently held the view that anyone who took his own life must be ill and therefore was not to blame.

Beneath the grey November sky, with the wind whipping cold across the hills, uncle Walter was buried with all the words, with tears and with prayers. To outward eyes his family must have looked suitably grief-stricken and it was only my new-found cynicism which said they were acting a part. I saw the brass plate, with his name engraved. Some stray gleam of light briefly erased the words and when they appeared again they said, ' Romaine Faulkner '.

The darkness came back across my eyes. I don't even remember falling.

I was cold, so cold, shivering and shuddering, coming back from the edges of limbo to the shadows of the church porch. I lay on one of the stone seats and beyond the archway people were grouped, trying to look as though they weren't curious.

" It's all right, love," Tom's voice breathed beside me. " You'll be all right."

His coat covered me like a blanket, but I was still cold, my teeth chattering. I was cold inside, deep inside, as though I were waking after centuries.

He helped me to sit up and I held my whirling head, leaning on him. It had been like that day in church, when the warning came, except that it had been twice as strong. I had seen my own name written on a coffin lid.

" What is it?" Tom asked anxiously, chafing my hands. " What happened?"

" She fainted," Peter said tersely from behind him. " What do you think happened? I'll take her now, Jamieson."

Tom leapt to his feet and I saw his hand clenching and unclenching at his side as he said in a low, furious voice, " No, you won't, Faulkner! I don't want to make a scene. Just go with your mother. I'll bring Romaine."

" You'll regret this," Peter muttered between his teeth, but he turned on his heel and pushed through the dispersing crowd.

As Tom helped me to my feet, his mother and Connan appeared outside the porch. Ruth's eyes were red and swollen, and there was still about her a look of the girl in plaits. I hardly dared look at her for fear she would read the knowledge in my eyes.

" How is she?" she asked.

" I'm not sure," Tom said, and I could hear the concern in his voice. " Did you see? She suddenly went pale as a sheet and dropped, like a felled oak."

The words struck me like a blow and I winced, remembering the trees in Devil's Wood—oak trees.

" What's wrong?" Tom asked anxiously, bending to look at my face. " Are you in pain?"

" I'm just cold," I said, my teeth chattering uncontrollably. " I want to go home, Tom. Please take me home." In my mind, momentarily, ' home ' was a white house by the Seine, where my father would be waiting. The shock of realising that brought me entirely back to reality.

With Tom's coat around me and his arm over that, I was led down the path, through the lych gate to where his car was parked on the verge. The Faulkner Rolls had already gone. They would not be pleased about any of this, I was sure, though it didn't seem to matter much. On this terrible day nothing mattered.

As Tom opened the door of his car, someone called, " Mrs. McIver! Wait, please," and Dick Handley came from the lych gate, where Evan stood with his surplice billowing round him. Beside him, Jill was a slender figure in long black skirt and cloak.

" Could I have a word with you?" Dick asked of Ruth, taking her arm. " It won't take long, but it is rather important."

" Oh, can't it . . . " Tom began, starting after his mother. He was stopped by Connan's hand on his arm.

" Leave it, Tom," the old man said gravely.

I clutched the car door, trembling, watching Evan and Dick speaking solemnly to Ruth. She glanced back once at Tom and Connan, seeming agitated.

" What's going on?" Tom demanded impatiently. " We ought to get Romaine home."

" It doesn't matter," I said.

" But it does. Look at you—you're still shaking. Sit in the car, love."

I shook my head, my eyes on the trio by the gate. I knew with cold certainty what it was they were discussing, on this day of all days, uncle Walter's friend, the vicar, and the woman who had been uncle Walter's mistress. I dreaded what was about to happen, but I wanted to be part of it. Almost without my being aware of it, my hand crept into Tom's and he looked at me sharply, seeing my tears.

"I love you, Tom," I breathed. "Whatever happens, remember that."

"Nothing's going to happen," he replied, touching my cold face with an equally cold hand. "You just need to rest, that's all."

He had misunderstood what I meant, but I didn't correct him for Ruth was coming back, slowly and wearily, her eyes on the ground.

"Mother?" Tom said in a puzzled voice.

"Let's go, Tom," she sighed.

He wanted to ask questions, I could see, but instead he saw me into the front passenger seat and strode round to take his place behind the wheel, while his mother and Connan climbed into the back. In a silence that sang with unasked questions, we drove to Falconsgarth.

"Tom . . ." Ruth said as the car stopped in the drive. "Go in with Romaine, love. Stay with her. We'll walk home."

"I've made enough trouble for one day," Tom said.

"I mean it, Tom. Reverend Bland and Mr. Handley 'specially asked that you should be there. They're going to read the Will. You ought to be there." Her voice was quiet and calm, but managed to express so much heart-ache that I hurt for her.

I saw Tom squint in the rear-view mirror before he turned to face her, his arm hooked over the back of the seat. "*I* did?"

"Yes, love. He's left you something. He's left you . . . the turnip watch."

Tom started to say something, stopped, frowned, and was silent, his eyes on his mother. I could see the thoughts racing behind those eyes, but otherwise there was little expression on his face.

"The turnip watch always goes to the oldest son," he said eventually, as if repeating a litany.

"Yes, Tom." From the corner of my eye I saw her clutch Connan's hand tightly.

"I see," Tom said with a sigh. "He couldn't let well alone, could he? I suppose they know?" He glanced at me questioningly. "You knew?"

I ran my tongue round my parched lips, croaking, "Only since yesterday. I found an album he had kept secretly. I've hidden it. I wasn't sure who knew. Tom . . . are you angry?"

"I'm not even very surprised," he said with a smile that had no amusement in it. "Now that I know, it seems I've suspected for a long time. Walter was always far too nice to me. Shall we go?"

He shouldn't be this calm, I thought worriedly. Was there going to be an explosion when he encountered the family?

As I climbed out into the cold wind, Dick's ancient car rattled to a halt behind us. Out of it came Dick and Evan.

Behind me, Connan said, "Keep your head, son. It's not that important."

"I know," said Tom, taking my arm.

Dick led the way, surprisingly taking charge. We found the family gathered in the big drawing room with its elegant blue and white decor touched with gold. They were taking tea. On a side table a small buffet had been arranged for anyone who might come back to the house. Apart from ourselves and the family lawyer, who stood by the table like a thin black crow, no one had come for the funeral repast.

Our entrance caused the family to freeze momentarily, and it was grandmother who recovered first, walking with her head held high across the wide expanse of carpet, slender and petite in her black dress with a double row of pearls.

"Are you feeling better, Romaine?" she enquired worriedly. "Sit down, my dear. Gentlemen . . . thank you for coming. Will you have some tea?"

Wanting to scream, I wandered to a chair and sat down, catching sight of aunt Lydia's face. She was staring at the three men as if she had never seen them before. Behind her, Peter was glowering at Tom.

"Lady Faulkner," Dick said heavily. "I don't know if you're aware of it, but Walter made Reverend Bland and myself his executors."

"Did he?" She sounded surprised, fingering her pearls. "But he had nothing to leave of any value. Really ... there's no need to put yourselves out. Unfortunately, we have not yet found the Will. Mr. Landrow," with a gesture at the lawyer, "has not been asked to keep one."

"I'm aware of that," Dick said, reaching into his inside pocket for a long brown envelope. "Walter left his Will with me. As you probably know, I qualified as a solicitor, though I don't practise any more. Walter's instructions were for me to read the Will on the day of his funeral and then come to Falconsgarth and make sure you all knew about it."

"Well, that's a relief!" my aunt said. "Trust Walter to do things in a roundabout way. May I see it?"

"Don't you know what's in it?" Dick asked.

Aunt Lydia blinked at him, failing to understand what the atmosphere was pregnant with. She didn't know about Tom, I thought with a catch in my throat. And neither did Peter.

"Well, read it!" grandmother said fiercely. "Read it, since you're determined to do this."

Dick looked uncomfortable. Evan was scratching his chin unhappily. And Tom stood, tall and elegant in his dark suit and tie, hands linked in front of him, eyes fixed on the middle distance without a flicker of emotion—like a man going to the scaffold, I thought.

In a low, clear voice, Dick began to read the preamble, " ... being of sound mind ... hereby bequeath as follows." He paused to clear his throat. "To my son Thomas Michael, known as Jamieson ... "

"What?" Peter snapped, and my aunt gave a curious gasp and bit her knuckles.

"Go on," grandmother said with subdued fury. "Read it out! Aloud!"

"... the traditional heirloom of the turnip watch, of beaten silver, dated eighteen fifty-six. In acknowledgement of him as my older son and heir ..."

"My God!" Peter got out. "He's given him a claim to the estate! He can't do that! Grandmother ..."

She was watching Tom, waiting for some reaction from him, and he slowly turned his eyes towards her, a faint, bitter smile twisting one corner of his mouth.

"I don't want it," he said steadily. "I don't want any part of it. I wouldn't sleep if I did this, and I value my sleep. You see, Lady Faulkner, I have a conscience. Please excuse me."

Unable to let him go like that, I fled after him into the hall, closing the door behind me. "Tom!"

He stopped, his back turned to me, waiting.

"Please, Tom, talk to me. What are you thinking?"

"I'm thinking that I shall be glad to get home and have some tea," he said slowly swinging round to face me. "I'm wondering if Walter cared what this would do to my mother —and to his wife and son—his legitimate son. This was the coward's way, when he would be safely out of it."

"And for yourself?" I asked worriedly. "What do you feel for yourself?"

He shrugged, grey eyes steady on mine. "Nothing. Nothing at all. It doesn't mean a thing to me. For thirty years I've had no father. I learned to accept that. But I have a mother I care about, and I have Con. I have a home, a career, a life of my own. All of this," his gesture encompassed the house, "is an irrelevancy, to me personally. What did you expect?"

I stared at him blankly, amazed by his reaction—which was no reaction at all. "I'm not sure. All this time you've hated the Faulkners and now ... you're one of them."

"So was your father," he reminded me. "That didn't stop him from walking out, and he had been part of all this. I'm not, nor do I want to be. Whoever the man was who participated in my conception, I am myself—Tom Jamieson. I don't intend to change."

Behind me in the drawing room a furore had broken out, voices raised, but in the hall there was a stillness. Tom's calmness bewildered me, but as I began to accept that he meant what he said there was pride in me for his strength and maturity.

"I'm just myself," Tom said again. "Halliday's cowman, remember?"

"Yes," I breathed. "How angry you were when I said that."

"Well, I'm proud of what I've achieved. It isn't much, but it's more than some men have. And some day I'm going to have my own farm, and take mother and Con away from the shadow of Falconsgarth. That's what I've always dreamed of doing—getting right away from the Faulkners." The bitter smile touched his mouth again. "It's ironic, isn't it? Wherever I go, I take part of the Faulkners with me. Faulkner blood runs in my veins, but thank God I'm free from Faulkner spite and Faulkner greed. I've seen what that can do to people."

Despite his outward acceptance, I realised, he had been hurt by that day's revelation. Perhaps he himself didn't know it yet.

"He loved your mother," I said. "And he loved you, too. Very much. You can see it in the way he cherished the photographs I found. I'll bring the album to you. You ought to have it, at least to see it. It meant a great deal to him."

"Then why did he marry Lydia?" he asked, and shrugged. "Not that I care. Mum would never have fitted in here. She'd have shrivelled and grown hard, like Lydia. I much prefer it the way it is . . . I must go. God knows what Mum's thinking. That's what I care about, Romaine—what exists at that cottage. As long as that's all right, nothing can really touch me."

"A safe harbour," I whispered. "Yes, I know what you mean."

For me there was no safe harbour. I had never known a

home filled with the kind of love that shone at the cottage. My father I had had, when he wasn't working and when mother was away, but when mother was there I had felt excluded from their circle. Now father and mother were both gone and I had no one, only the uneasy relationship with the Faulkners—only the dread that loomed over Falconsgarth, and the vision of my own name on a coffin lid.

Faced abruptly with my own aloneness, I could no longer stand to be with Tom. I fled from him, to run up the stairs with tears bursting from my eyes, and though he called my name I did not pause until I reached my room.

The pain in my side was intense as I lay on my bed. The car accident had smashed four of my ribs and punctured my lung and now I felt almost as bad as I had when I awoke after the operation which pieced me together. Perhaps something had gone wrong inside me. Perhaps that was how the curse would work on me. I dreamed uneasily of my grandfather Dupris, walking on the hills proudly showing me his vines, which were at all withered and dying.

When I woke the pain had almost gone and I could breathe more easily. I must have wrenched myself when I fainted. I rationalised, and then cried so bitterly I had strained my lung. I had been trying to do too much, pretending I was completely fit again when actually it would be some time before my health was normal. Small wonder that I reached out for Tom's warmth and strength, seeing in him the comfort and support I needed.

I took a refreshing shower and went down to dinner, only to find aunt Lydia absent from the table.

" She wasn't hungry," grandmother explained when I enquired. " Can you wonder at it? To be told, after thirty years of marriage, that her husband had an illegitimate son . . . I only hope Walter is aware of the misery he caused."

" I'll bet he's laughing his head off," Peter said acidly. " It makes me ill when I think of him and Ruth McIver . . . "

" She wasn't Ruth McIver then," grandmother pointed out. " She was Ruth Jamieson, just the young daughter of

our ploughman, and your father was a young fool—younger
than you are now."

Peter's mouth curved as if he felt sick. "And you knew?
Then you knew Jamieson had a claim to the estate, if he ever
found out. When he has a chance to think about it . . . He'd
be a fool not to claim."

In grandmother's eyes there was a spark formed of amusement and determination. "I'm not dead yet, Peter," she said
pertly. "I don't intend to die for some years, and before I do
we'll have Mr. Jamieson repeat in writing what he said yesterday. I think you underestimate him. He has his own kind of
pride. He'll write the letter."

They seemed to have forgotten I was there. I detested them
for cold-bloodedly planning to make Tom cut himself off
from any inheritance to which he might be entitled, though
the laws governing these things were a mystery to me and I
could not tell if such a letter would have any legal value. Still,
he had made it very clear that he wanted nothing from
Falconsgarth.

I understood now why grandmother had torn up that latest
photograph of Tom. I could imagine her confronting uncle
Walter in the study, tearing the picture to shreds in front of
him, contemptuously. But at least she had not known about
his secret album, and if I had my way she would never
know.

Immediately after dinner I went to my room, to sit in bed
reading my uncle's stories. They were rather rambling and
ill-formed, but fascinating because of what they revealed of
the writer, as he unconsciously poured out his feelings of
guilt and despair. I wondered if he had realised how much
of himself he had put into the stories, for from them I discovered that he had hated his wife and feared his mother, and
that Peter had been a stranger to him, as though he were
someone else's child. The emotions lay open on the page,
naked and bleeding.

So the faults had not all been on the family's side. Uncle
Walter had done his share towards destroying his own re-

lationships with his wife and son. If it had been difficult for him, so it must have been difficult for aunt Lydia and Peter, she married to a man who was secretly yearning for someone else, and he the son of an indifferent father. He must have felt about his father as I had felt about my mother—excluded, for reasons neither of us understood.

Strangely, after the traumatic day I slept deeply and if dreams came they were gone when I woke to a bright, crisp morning. The trees of The Wood were sharply outlined against the sky and the air was so clear I felt I could see every twig and notch. Testing my ribs, I found them less sore, though the fear was still there across the back of my mind, the hovering dark mist that presaged danger, and I had lost the glow which had been returning to my skin when I first came to Falconsgarth. In my own mind I was convinced that my personal doom was near at hand. There was no way in which I could avoid it.

" Am I late?" I asked, finding Peter alone at breakfast.

" No one else is up yet," he told me. " We were late to bed. There was a lot to talk about."

I helped myself to toast and coffee and sat next to him, glancing at the paper he had open on the table. " What's happening in the world?"

" The usual. Don't try to make conversation, Romaine. I don't feel much like small-talk."

" Is it small-talk to say . . . I wish we could be friends, Peter. I know how you must be feeling. What happened yesterday . . . it was terrible. Tom realised that, too. He knew it would be a shock for you and your mother."

" Oh, did he?" He folded the paper and tossed it to the floor, turning to look at me bitterly. " So now I must appreciate his sensitivity, must I? Just because he's my half-brother? You don't seem to appreciate that because of him my mother now knows her marriage was a sham and I know that to my father I was a poor replica of someone I detest. Do you expect me to welcome him with open arms?"

" No. But you might try to see that it was hard for him,

too. Why do you dislike him so much? What has he ever done to you?"

"Done? You mean apart from hating us all this time, and showing it at every opportunity? And seducing you?"

"He hasn't seduced me," I objected.

"Not physically, maybe. Not yet. Come to think of it, I understand that one of your objections to me was the fact of our close relationship. Has it occurred to you that Jamieson is your cousin, too?"

It had not occurred to me, but it didn't make any difference. "You said yourself that you can't decide when to fall in love."

"And *you* said you didn't intend to let it happen for a while yet. Changed your mind in a hurry, didn't you? Is it the ' real thing'? When have you had the time to get to know anything about him?"

"I know more about him than I know about you," I replied.

"Oh, really? You amaze me. What are you, psychic?"

"Sometimes I think so," I said. "Not about people, but ... Peter will you give up on The Wood now? Hasn't enough happened to ..."

He got up abruptly and strode towards the door. "Not that again! Spare me that! I'm going out. There's a girl I want to see. Have a lovely day."

When I had seen him drive away, I went to the library to use the phone and called Paris, talking briefly to my friend Marie-Elise, telling her a little truth and quite a few lies; then I called mother's lawyer, who said he would be sending me some papers to sign. We talked in rapid French, so if anyone happened to be listening on the extension it was doubtful if the conversation could be followed.

As I left the library, I encountered grandmother in the hall. For the first time since I had known her she looked tired, so the events of the last few days must have affected her as they had affected the rest of us."

"I've just been using the phone," I told her. "I checked

how much the calls cost and I'll give you the money directly. How are you feeling today?"

She gave me a wan smile. " I'm beginning to feel my age, my dear. Sometimes I forget that I shall be seventy in January. Have you breakfasted?"

"Yes, thank you. I'm going out—to the McIvers'. I know how you feel about them, but . . . "

" You must do as you please," she said, waving a pale hand in the air. " All my family defy me over the McIvers. No good has ever come of it, but you must learn from your own mistakes, I suppose. Yes, go. But take care of yourself."

Going to my room, I put uncle Walter's manuscripts in my overnight bag with the blue album, and with the bag slung over my shoulder I left the house by the back door.

There was thick frost crisping the leaves in the wood where the sun had not reached, and a silver covering in every shadow. I made my way through the middle of the woods, around the foot of the hill, walking slowly but steadily, my eyes on the ground.

When I emerged from the trees that other Wood loomed at the top of the bare hill to my left and I could see that the lightning-split tree had gone. Beside it there was a gap, where another great oak had stood, and as I stared at the place unhappily the cold, premonitory shadow touched my soul again. Whatever I told myself, and however bright the day, I *felt* the darkness which surrounded Devil's Wood, felt it in the deep instinctive areas of my being, even from this distance. And I knew that its menace was for me.

A line of washing billowed on the line behind the cottage as I took the path to the back door and knocked there, only to stand foolishly, unanswered. I tried three times, each time knocking louder, but there was no sound from inside the cottage. Depressed, I derided myself for the bold announcement I had made. Going to the McIvers', indeed!

I was about to leave when I heard the gate click. Connan's deep voice sounded faintly, talking in an undertone, and when he appeared round the corner of the cottage I saw that

he was apparently talking to his coat. He looked surprised to
see me, then he laughed.

"No, I've not gone queer in the head, lass. Look here what
I've got."

Inside his coat, curled up in a ball, was a speckled puppy
with bright eyes and long floppy ears. It licked my fingers
with a warm tongue and I laughed.

"He's lovely!"

"She," the old man corrected. "Come on in and you can
get acquainted."

The kitchen was as warm as I remembered, though on that
day it smelled of soap-powder. Ruth had done her washing
early.

"They've gone shopping," Connan told me. "Tom'll be
sorry to have missed you."

"Will he?"

He turned to survey me with grave blue eyes. "Do you
doubt it?"

"I don't know," I said unhappily, watching him set the
pup on the floor, where it began to sniff and explore. "Yesterday . . . oh, I suppose it was a peculiar day for all of us. How's
Ruth? Was she very upset?"

"Not after she'd talked to Tom. She was worried how he
would take it, but he's a sensible lad. Sit down, Romaine."

I pulled a chair from beneath the table, setting my bag on
the floor, where the puppy came to investigate it, all enquiring
nose and joyous tail. "You knew, didn't you, Mr. McIver?
You knew about Tom."

"Aye. I knew from the start." Water gushed as he filled
the kettle and set it to boil before sitting opposite me.
"Walter would have married Ruth if it hadn't been for that
interfering old witch at Falconsgarth. Couldn't have her son
marrying the ploughman's daughter, could she? So when
Ruth had to confess to her father that she'd fallen for a child,
he sent her away. He knew it wasn't any use going to Falconsgarth and demanding that Walter do the right thing . . . Hey!
Stop that!"

He was too late. The pup had puddled on the floor. When Connan shouted it looked up at him with a comical stare of astonishment that made me laugh and I bent to pet the little dog, which licked my hand enthusiastically.

It was strange, I thought as the old man got a cloth and some disinfectant; I felt at home here. Everything was so normal. I could not remember ever having laughed at Falconsgarth.

"Wretch!" said Connan, shaking his finger at the pup as he resumed his chair. "Oh, Ruth'll bind. But I couldn't resist her. Since Maidie . . . Have you ever had a dog?"

I shook my head, gently pulling the pup's ear as I straightened in the chair. "Mother didn't like animals. Mr. McIver . . . go on with what you were saying—about Ruth and uncle Walter."

"There's not a lot to say. They were both too young. She was sixteen and he was twenty. His mother threatened to disinherit him if he didn't stop seeing Ruth, and she introduced him to Lydia, making her intentions clear. They were married a month after Tom was born."

The kettle was boiling and he got up to make two cups of instant coffee, placing them on the table.

"But Ruth wasn't in Winterford when Tom was born?" I queried.

"No. She was in Ilfracombe, with her great-aunt. Near enough for Walter to visit. Then young Peter came along and things seemed to die a natural death. Ruth came back here a few years later, after her father passed on, but of course she never told Tom the truth. He thought his father was someone in Ilfracombe."

Reaching for the bag, I took out the album and gave it to him silently, watching as he flicked through a few pages and sighed.

"Aye, I did wonder what he was doing with them. He always told Tom he was practising photography—testing his camera and that. Do you want Tom to have this?"

"That's up to him, and Ruth. The photographs are worth

saving, if nothing else. And there are some manuscripts—
stories my uncle wrote. No one at Falconsgarth wants them."

Connan folded his arms on the table, leaning towards me
with an intent stare. "You seem depressed, Romaine. What's
the trouble?"

"What isn't? . . . What happened at The Wood? Tom said
you had the impression the men were scared away. Did *you*
scare them?"

"Me?" He shook his grey head, scratching his beard.
"Not me. They just took off. One of them said, 'You can
keep the place. We won't be back.' Well, I was busy at the
time and it soon got dark, so I didn't get up there until the
next day. Do you fancy a walk? We can take this young imp
with us. Do her good to have a run."

I put my coat on and waited while he fixed a lead to the
pup's collar. 'Young imp,' I thought. That was what my
father used to call me. Had he got the expression from
Connan McIver?

"It's a good clean day," Connan remarked, sniffing the
biting wind. "Here, take my arm, lass. Tom'll not forgive me
if I don't take good care of you. We'll take it slow up the hill."

"Why did my father leave Falconsgarth?" I asked abruptly.
"You wouldn't tell me the first day I was here, but I want to
know. Someone said he didn't get on with grandmother."

He watched the rough grass pass under our feet for a
moment, and spoke sharply to the puppy which was pulling
at the lead. "No, he didn't. I don't know that it's my place
to tell you about that."

"Then who will? I was going to ask my uncle, but . . . And
I don't want grandmother's version. I want the truth."

He gave me a surprised glance. "You've learned something, I see. But everyone has his own version of the truth.
No doubt mine's as prejudiced as any. What is it you want
to know?"

"Everything! Why did he leave his home? Why did he
tell me there was no one who mattered to him left at Falconsgarth?"

"That's probably how he felt," Connan said slowly. "It was her as drove him out—his mother. When I first knew her ... She was a little slip of a thing. Eighteen, she was, and him in his thirties. She was a fortune-hunter if ever I saw one. Later on I told Gerald so, and he laughed, but he must have told her because from then on she acted like I was dirt.

"Well, they went away—him being in the Army and his father still alive, then when the war came she and the boys settled here and I got to know William—your father. His mother favoured her older boy, who would be the heir, and William felt left out. He used to come and tell me about it, and as he grew older so he got more bitter. Then there was all the trouble over Ruth. A couple of years later, Gerald died— your grandfather, that is. Went quite suddenly. If you ask me, he was the only reason William had stayed so long. Without him, there wasn't anything for the lad to stay for."

"So he just went away?" I asked.

"Not right then, not immediately, no. He was still hoping things might change between him and his mother. She sacked me, for no good reason except that she'd always hated me, and William took my side. And then she started planning to fell Devil's Wood. That was the last straw as far as William was concerned. They had one final row and he walked out."

"But she didn't cut The Wood, not then," I said.

"No. Changed her mind for some reason, but six years ago she tried again. You know what happened. And you'll soon see what happened this time."

We were almost level with the fence. Connan tied the puppy's lead to the unsteady structure and himself clambered over into the undergrowth, helping me to follow.

"Now be careful," he advised. "It's full of pot-holes. See how that tree fell?"

The second tree, which had been alive when it was cut, had toppled into The Wood, breaking the branches of other trees as it fell. The men had denuded it of its lower branches, which lay forlornly in our path, some of them under the bole

E

of the felled oak. Even I could see that the workmen had made a messy job of it.

"It should have fallen outwards," Connan told me in a hushed voice. "One of them was nearly crushed. They were frightened, Romaine."

Moving slowly, we negotiated the lopped branches. In among the trees there were holly bushes and a few brown-leaved hazels, growing small and stunted among grass and trailing briars. Overhead the branches leaned together as if protecting the place from the light, so that only vagrant gleams of sunlight slanted among the tangle. The cold stillness seemed aware, as if The Wood were holding its breath, waiting and watching. Not a bird flew or sang.

My instincts were screaming at me to fly from the aura of evil that I could almost smell. It breathed very strong here, vibrating along my nerves. I was aware of every twig, every fallen leaf. Invisible eyes seemed to stare at me from behind the lacework of branches and every tiny hair on my body had stiffened, prickling all over my skin.

"Connan!" I breathed.

He glanced round, his own eyes sombre. "Brave it, lass. Only you will understand."

His voice had regained its mystic quality and like one hypnotised I closed my mind to the threat that beat in the very air and followed him, briars tearing at my slacks, reaching for my eyes.

In the centre of the copse, where the top of the felled tree had reached, there were thick shadows, seeming to gather round a peculiarly-shaped hummock, ridden with weeds and trailing fronds. It was too regular to be natural, and beneath the wild growth there were dark planes which appeared to be stone. The very top branches of the tree had struck this object.

It was a tomb. Six feet away, the knowledge came cold into my brain. I saw rectangular outlines beneath the creeping weeds. The falling tree had shattered one corner of it, and someone had pulled away the trailers from the top. Trembling, I forced myself to go nearer, knowing that the mark of Fate was on me and that this place was its source.

The tomb was green with lichen, pitted and scarred by time, but the carving on the top was still clear. It leered up at me—a face with horns and a long tongue flicking to one side.

I heard the undergrowth rustle as Connan pushed through to stand by the head of the tomb. "There's a name on it here," he said. "Ricard Falconer."

"Ricard . . . " I got out through a dark veil across my mind. "He was hanged as a witch, and buried . . . buried secretly . . . "

"Secret, and unsanctified," Connan added in tones of doom. "Can you read what it says under the carving?"

With shaking fingers I traced the worn letters, clearer in reality than they had been in the photograph—d, i, a, b, *Diabolo suo*. "Something about the devil?"

"Aye," Connan said. "I went and asked the vicar last night. It says, 'Ricard Falconer. To the devil his own.'"

NINE

I did not feel safe until we were back inside the warm cottage and even then I was still shaking with nerves which almost made me spill the fresh coffee Connan made. In a basket on the floor the puppy snuffled, curling itself for sleep. We had found it whining pitifully, straining to break away from its tether as if it, too, sensed the malevolence of The Wood.

"I'm sorry, lass," Connan said, watching me with anxious

blue eyes. "But I had to show you. You're a Faulkner. You can do something about it."

"*I* can?" My laugh was unsteady. "Such as what?"

"Talk to the vicar. He might be able to help. Exorcism, or some such thing. What's in that wood has to be got rid of."

"But what does it mean?"

"You know that as well as I do. He was hanged for a witch. Even his family must have believed it or they wouldn't have given him that epitaph. Maybe he died with a curse on his lips. Who knows? But you felt the vibrations, didn't you? There's something wicked lying over that wood, something age-old and evil that's slowly destroying the Faulkners every time they try to disturb it. And now the tomb is broken."

This is nonsense! part of me was protesting. This old man is a witch himself, casting his spell on you. Grandmother said he was our enemy, remember?

But the cottage was cosy; Connan himself was a kindly man with worried blue eyes; and the shadow was there, across my mind, obliterating my future.

"Why should you care, after the way they treated you?" I asked him. "After what they've done to Ruth, and to Tom . . ."

"Not all the Faulkners are bad," he said with a slow smile. "Your grandfather was my friend, and so was your father. Walter was weak, but he wasn't evil. And now there's you . . . There's no mending what's past. I'm too old to care any more about that. Young Tom cares more than I do."

"When will he be home?" I asked.

"There's no telling. Ruth's a terror when she gets in the shops. But I'll tell them you came. Tom'll be pleased to know you're all right. He was worried about you yesterday. And he was shaken-up, you know, whatever he might have said."

"Yes, I know." I stood up, sparing a smile for the peaceful puppy. "I think I will go and talk to Evan. He'll probably tell me I'm crazy, but I can try."

As I opened the door, a wave of relief and gladness swept

through me, for Ruth was coming round the corner, a bulging shopping bag over one arm, and behind her was Tom, laden with two more baskets. Ruth paused on seeing me, looking at me uncertainly, and in her eyes I saw all the misery she must have endured and the question about what I felt for her now that I knew her history.

Impulsively, I went to her and kissed her, hoping to convey my understanding. "Hello, Ruth. How are you?"

"I'm fine," she said with a smile that countered the misty tears in her eyes. "Get the kettle on, Con."

"I was just on my way," I said as she went into the cottage. I glanced at Tom, myself uncertain. "I mustn't stay any longer. I've been here nearly all morning. Are you all right?"

He had been standing like a statue, but he suddenly came to life, putting down the baskets, taking two quick strides towards me, his mouth seeking mine passionately, achingly, and I clung to him, weeping with relief. Behind me, the cottage door quietly closed.

"This is ridiculous," Tom muttered roughly, his lips buried in my hair, his arms tightly about me. "You worry about me, and I worry about you. Don't go back to France. Stay here with me. To hell with the family. I love you."

"Oh, Tom!" I managed, lifting my lips to his again, glorying in the strength of him. Something in the back of my mind was protesting that this was madness, that there were too many obstacles between us, but I also knew with a deadly certainty that there might not be too much time left for me and I recklessly threw myself into any joy I might have before the doom I feared overcame me.

In that same mood of frantic abandonment, I allowed myself to be persuaded to stay for lunch, and Tom drove me to the phone box in the village because he didn't want me to have to go back to Falconsgarth and have grandmother show her disapproval. So I spoke to aunt Lydia on the phone and told her I would not be in for lunch, while Tom blew in my ear and made me laugh.

We fell out of the phone box into the village street, laughing like idiots, and ran hand in hand back to the car, which was a stupid thing to do because it made the pain come back in my side.

"You should have said," Tom told me worriedly.

"I keep forgetting. Didn't you realise you had an invalid on your hands? Do you want an invalid?"

"I want you," he said, grey eyes tender with love. "I'll take care of you, even when you're well again. I don't ever want to see you look the way you looked yesterday. You frightened me half to death, fainting that way."

The shadow came back across my happiness, but I willed it away. Not yet. Not yet. I'll face it when it comes, but not yet.

Over lunch, Connan and I told them what we had found in the copse. Ruth was worried and Tom was sceptical, but he agreed to come with me to see Evan.

"He'll be at the Christmas Fair this afternoon," Ruth told us. "In the W. I. hall. You can catch him there and ask him. Do you think he'll come?"

"All I can do is ask," I said. "By the way, did Connan show you the album? I hope I did the right thing, bringing it, but it would have grieved uncle Walter to think it was thrown away."

"You did right," Ruth told me. "Some of those pictures I've never seen. They'll be nice to keep. Here, Tom, look." She fetched the album and gave it to Tom, who took it without comment and began to look through it.

"There are stories, too," Ruth added. "You can look at them when you've time."

He laid the album aside, said, "Yes, I will," indifferently, and went to kneel by the puppy, picking it up and stroking its head. "Where did you get her, Con?"

"The Harrisons' bitch had a litter. Father was a spaniel, by the looks of it."

"As if I didn't have enough to do without cleaning up after a pup," Ruth sighed, but from her face I guessed she didn't really mind.

Tom brought the pup to me, placing it on my lap where

it wobbled unsteadily before planting heavy paws on my breast and rasping its tongue along my chin.

" She's cute, don't you think?" Tom asked, laughing as he knelt beside me. " What are you calling her, Con?"

" I hadn't thought of it," the old man said, lighting his pipe. " Let Romaine choose a name."

Smiling, Tom looked up at me. " What do you think?

" I really don't know," I said, still trying to avoid the puppy's affectionate advances.

He considered the dog, stroking its flank so that it dropped onto all fours and watched him expectantly. " She's got brown eyes, like you. Gypsy? That's a good name for her."

" How *did* you know about that?" I asked.

" Con told me."

" And how did he know?" I asked the old man.

" From Walter. What did you think—that I was a mind-reader?"

" Or a warlock," I said lightly, still fighting with my own inner darkness.

The dog's name stuck. From then on she was ' Gypsy ', which amused Tom hugely. He called her by name at every opportunity, sending sly, laughing glances at me.

Since Evan was due to perform the opening ceremony at the W.I. Christmas Fair at two thirty that afternoon, we delayed until about three before going to the hall. The place was crammed with people crowding round the stalls, which were selling home-made toys, tea-cosies, cushions ... Tinsel streamers crossed the ceiling in gaudy array. There was even a Father Christmas with a bran tub.

We spotted Evan in the far corner by the tea-stall, but as we were pushing through the throng a voice hailed me and I looked round to see Mrs. Wells struggling between two large ladies who were craning to see the wares.

" Miss Faulkner! " she gasped, gaining my side. " How very kind of you to come. It's not often we're honoured by supporters from Falconsgarth. Did you find the time to mention our problem to Lady Faulkner? Will she help?"

"I'm working on it," I said. "If the negotiations for the sale haven't gone too far, I'll get it stopped."

"You will?" she said blankly. "How?"

"Oh, I have my contacts. I should be able to let you know by . . . this time next week." The hesitation came with the thought that I might not be there at this time next week. There was no telling how long it would be before it happened. Days. Hours.

Stammering her bewildered thanks, Mrs. Wells returned to work and I looked round for Tom, who had been in front of me when I stopped. For one awful moment I thought I had lost him, then I saw him smiling at me, shouldering through the crowd of buyers, bringing me a lop-eared rabbit made of pink felt. It had a drunken grin and crossed eyes, but it was very appealing.

"That's your good-luck charm," he told me. "Pre-Christmas present."

Tears misted my eyes as I looked at the pink rabbit. Christmas was a long time away, five weeks, or perhaps never, for me. I hugged the silly thing and reached up to kiss Tom's cheek, unaware of the people around us until Evan's voice said, "Hello, you two."

It was clear from his expression that he had not expected to find us there, certainly not together as we so obviously were.

"We came to see you, Evan," I said. "Is there somewhere we could talk?"

"Only outside. Let me make a passage for you."

The sun was being swallowed by a cloud and there was a hint of returning mist in the air as we left the heat of the crowded hall and grouped by the iron railing, on the unkempt grass that filled the plot.

Evan glanced from my face to Tom's glumly. "If it's about yesterday . . ."

"It's not," I interrupted. "Evan . . . you remember what I asked you about last Monday, when I came to the vicarage?"

His eyes held a puzzled expression as again he glanced at Tom. "Yes. You asked about The Wood. Does this have something to do with Mr. McIver? What has he been telling you, Romaine?"

"He didn't tell me; he showed me. He asked you what ' *Diabolo suo* ' meant, didn't he?"

"He did, and very mysterious he was, too. Wouldn't tell me why, or where he'd seen it."

"He saw it in Devil's Wood," I said, clasping Tom's hand tightly. "There's a tomb there—Ricard Falconer's tomb. The witch, you remember? There's something . . . some evil. Connan and I both felt it. Is there some ceremony you could perform—exorcism, or something similar?"

He sent Tom a look which said little for my mental state.

"I'm not imagining things!" I cried. "Evan, my father and my uncle are both dead because of the curse, not to mention Ned Freeman. And the workmen were frightened away because the tree they were felling went the wrong way and cracked the tomb. It meant something. There *is* a force! . . . Oh, humour me, if that's the way it must be, but please do something!"

"You won't persuade her otherwise," Tom said, shaking his head. "Nor Con, either. Maybe they can sense things we can't. Anyway, Mr. Bland, we'd be grateful if you could do something. The church does have a service of this kind, doesn't it?"

Evan was looking unhappy. "Well, yes, but it isn't used very often. I shall have to have a word with my bishop about it, though I can't promise anything. But I can see you're serious, Romaine. I'll do what I can. Now if you'll excuse me I must get back to the fête. I'm supposed to make the draw for the raffle. I'll . . . be in touch."

"Make it soon, Evan," I begged him. "Please hurry."

As he returned to the hall, I knew with resignation that he did not understand.

"He thinks I'm mad, doesn't he?" I said as Tom and I walked away. "Do you think so, too?"

"I think there are things about you I shall never understand," Tom replied. "But if you feel so strongly then I'm behind you all the way. If he can stop you worrying ... Since when have you been on first-name terms with him, by the way? And how come you went to the vicarage?"

"Who else could I turn to? At the time, I was being torn in two, trying not to believe the legend. But more and more, during this week, I've been convinced. There have been signs and portents. Don't laugh at me, Tom."

He pulled me into his arms, holding me close against him with his cheek on my brow. "I never felt less like laughing in my life!" he muttered. "You're beginning to convince me, too."

When eventually I returned to Falconsgarth, Peter was there having tea with his mother in the red sitting room. I gathered that they had been discussing me, for when I went in the talk stopped and I became the object of severe glances.

"Well, look who it is," Peter said heavily. "The traitor in our midst. Have you had a lovely day with the family by-blow, Romaine?"

"If you mean Tom," I replied, keeping my temper with difficulty, "yes, I've had a very pleasant day."

Aunt Lydia's mouth turned sickly. "I don't know how you can. Knowing what he is ... "

"And what is he?" I interrupted. "What happened wasn't his fault. He wants nothing from any of you, which only proves he's probably the most decent and honourable member of the Faulkner family still living."

"Hah!" Peter exclaimed with a bark of laughter. "That's gratitude for you. That's the thanks we get for taking in the poor orphan."

The door behind me opened and grandmother came in, unsmiling. "So you're home at last, Romaine. Have you had tea?"

"Yes, thank you. Mrs. McIver made some just before I left. I'm going to have a bath and get changed. Tom's taking me out to dinner tonight. I know it's a little soon after uncle Walter ... but we're only going for a meal. I'm sorry if you object."

"We don't object," grandmother said. "Your life is your own, to ruin as you please. Where is he taking you?"

"I think he said Cheldonhoe."

"Green Valley Inn," Peter said flatly. "Trying to impress you, is he? Well, run along and get ready. Don't keep him waiting, whatever you do."

Under normal circumstances I would have hated the bitterness that was directed against me, but with time running out for me I didn't much care what they thought. I wanted to spend every moment with Tom.

During those last two frantic weeks when I had been touring England with mother, she had bought me an expensive evening ensemble which I had never worn. Bathed and perfumed, I put it on that evening, the long skirt in midnight blue with a frilled blouse in oyster silk. There was a cloak to match, lined with the silk, and I wore a pair of pearl earrings to complement the upswept hairstyle. Just for once I wanted Tom to see me at my best.

He was waiting in the car, having chosen not to enter the house where he knew he would be unwelcome.

"You look marvellous," he told me.

"So do you," I returned. "Oh, let's go, Tom. Let's get away from this place."

"I'm only too delighted to oblige," he said, putting the car into gear. "What sort of reception did you get?"

"Frosty."

"I was afraid of that. You must be the first person ever to disobey Lady Faulkner quite so openly. I just hope I'm not going to make life difficult for you. It's fine for me—I don't have to be at Falconsgarth. But you do."

"Not for long," I said, the words coming out before I could stop them. "I mean ... I'm only a temporary visitor. Oh, Tom, let's not talk about them. Tell me about yourself. I want to know everything about you."

" In one evening?" he queried with a grin. " There's more to me than that."

" I know." The words echoed through the emptiness in my soul. One evening might be all we had.

I began to understand why mother had behaved as she did in those days before the accident. She had known, as I did, that there was not much time left. I could sense the dark wings hovering over me, following behind the car no matter how fast we drove through the night, and suddenly I was aware of the million things I had hoped to do with my life, that would never be done now. So I clung to each minute, extracting the most from it.

We dined by candlelight, a wonderful meal with good wine, and I hardly let my eyes leave Tom's face, etching every angle and plane in my mind, recording his voice with all its nuances, loving him with every nerve and sinew because we were not going to have the years together that other people had. Every moment must be filled with memories to take with me into the loneliness ahead.

Afterwards, we hurried through the light drizzle and flung ourselves into the car, where Tom turned to me and touched my face in the darkness.

" Tell me what's wrong."

" Wrong?" I echoed.

" There's something. You're not usually this intense. Are you worried about what they'll say?"

" No! No, of course not. I'm . . . excited, that's all. I didn't think it could be like this."

" Is that the truth?"

" Yes! " My voice was too light, too breathy.

" You're not getting ready to give me the brush?"

" Tom! "

" Well, I wondered. We might get back to Falconsgarth and then you tell me kindly that it's no use, that it wouldn't work. Heaven knows we've got our problems, but there's nothing insurmountable, as long as we fight it together. That's what I believe, Romaine. Do you?"

"Of course!"

There was a moment's silence when I strained to see his face, but he was just a shadow.

"I thought our relationship was based on honesty," he said eventually. "I've always admired your quest for the truth. I admired your courage in going against the family . . ."

I reached out my hand, finding his shirt, letting my fingers curl round his neck as I leaned on him. "I'm not brave, Tom. I'm frightened. The truth . . . The truth is that if I had my way I would stay with you, from this moment on. I don't ever want to leave you."

He bent his head to press his lips on my hair, holding my head to his chest where I could hear the rapid thud of his heart.

"Then don't," he murmured. "I'll get a special licence. We'll be married before they can do anything to stop us. Mr. Halliday's got a farm cottage empty at the moment. We can move into that, away from the Faulkners, while I see about a mortgage for a place of our own. Even if we have to wait a while, it won't matter. We shall be together. We can work for the future. It won't be anything like Falconsgarth, but . . ."

Frantic, I stopped the words with my mouth, kissing him fiercely. I wanted to hear no more about a future I might never see.

"Yes, Tom," I breathed. "Yes, let's do that."

"You mean it?"

"Yes!" Of course I meant it. Perhaps I might be allowed a few more days, long enough to be married and have a little time with Tom before . . . For a moment the darkness closed right over me, shutting out the sight of the road along which we were travelling. There were not going to be days. The doom was coming nearer all the time.

Every nerve in me was alive, all my senses alert. We were taking a different route, along the edge of the coast, where the road swung at weird angles, climbing and descending, now a hairpin through a tiny wooded valley and now round the edge of a hill where I could hear the sea pounding below the woods that lined the steep cliff.

Although the darkness hid the details of the surrounding countryside, I knew that the drop to my left was fatally steep in some places, that a vehicle could plunge down through the slanting woods, and when our car filled suddenly with light from blazing headlamps right behind us, I knew the moment had come.

'No! Not Tom, too!' The prayer filled my mind. The following car began to overtake, though if it did it would put us over the edge. The black wings flapped in my ears. The edge came nearer . . .

TEN

For no apparent reason, the car behind us suddenly stopped and as its lights drew away in the distance there was plenty of room on the road. I heard Tom let out his breath in a great sigh of relief.

"Thank God for that! He must be drunk, the bloody fool! Are you all right?"

"I am now. I thought . . . "

"So did I," Tom said grimly.

He was concentrating on taking us out of danger, away from the coast road. Behind us now there was only darkness, no sign of the following car, and soon we were turning over a hill, heading inland again.

"He must have given himself a fright, too," Tom commented eventually. "That was a near thing, for all of us. And you . . . What did you mean, 'Not Tom, too'?"

" Did I say it aloud?"

" Say it? You screamed it. Don't you remember?"

" I thought I said it silently. It's not very clear in my mind. It had just occurred to me that you're a Faulkner, too, and the legend . . . " I bit my lip, but I had said too much.

Tom pulled the car into the side of the road, beneath the shelter of some trees, and switched on the interior light so that we could see each other.

" So that's it. That's what you're uptight about. Darling . . . " He sighed heavily, laying a gentle hand against my cheek. " What can I say? How do you argue with something so illogical?"

" You don't argue, Tom. You just accept that I have these feelings. My mother did, too. If I try to put it into words it sounds like mumbo-jumbo. There have been . . . warnings, and they're getting stronger. Unless we do something to counteract the power in The Wood . . . You see, it sounds stupid said aloud. I tried to tell Evan and he just thought I was cracked."

" Well, you're not." His finger ran the length of my nose and he leaned across to kiss me softly. " You're like Connan. Maybe you're a gypsy witch. Whatever you are, I love you very much."

" And I love you, Tom." I let my arms slide round his neck and burrowed close to the warmth of him. For a while there were no feelings except what I felt for him.

As the car moved off again, I let my head droop on the back of the seat. I felt drained now, but the pursuing dread had left me. It had been like a build-up of pressure that was released as soon as the other car stopped. The same thing had happened after uncle Walter died, I remembered. Would the premonition return again soon?

I shut the thought out, concentrating on watching Tom's classic profile lit by the backwash from the headlights. Some miracle had given us a little more time.

It was after midnight when we negotiated the pitch-dark drive to Falconsgarth, but there were still lights behind the curtains in the sitting room and as we stopped I saw the curtains move and someone look out briefly.

"They're waiting for me," I told Tom. "I'd better go. Shall I see you tomorrow? I'd like to go to church in the morning, but afterwards ..."

"I'll be here at ten fifteen," he said promptly. "We might as well go together and have a word with your friend Evan Bland. I think you have to wait three days after getting a special licence, so if I can get one on Monday . . . What's the matter? Second thoughts?"

"Not about marrying you," I assured him, laying my hand on his thigh. "The thing is ... I shall have to go back to France, if only briefly. There will be ends to tie up, and my flat to dispose of. Let me do that first, then I can concentrate on being your wife."

"You could do that after we're married, couldn't you? We could go to France for a honeymoon. I thought you wanted to get away from Falconsgarth."

"I do." A glance at the dark, looming house made me shiver. "Yes, I do. Give me a night to think about it, will you? I'll tell you in the morning. To be honest, I'm too tired to think straight at the moment."

"Fine. Just decide to say yes."

Parting reluctantly from him, I let myself into the house and went straight to the sitting room. Only grandmother was there, wearing a long pink dressing gown whose frilly collar set off her sweet face and white hair.

"You're very late," she said. "It's too bad of him to keep you out until this hour when he knows you aren't well."

"I'm feeling better every day," I replied. "Really, you needn't have waited up for me, grandmother."

"I know. But I worry about you." She gave me a little smile. "You're not a bad girl, are you? Just headstrong, like your father before you. Look, I've been keeping a hot drink for you in this pot." The 'pot' was an electric percolator standing on the hearth by the dying fire. She bent to pour its contents into a mug. "It's not coffee, it's chocolate.

Coffee's very bad for you at this time of night. There you are. Take this and get straight to bed. You look worn out again. I shall have to have a severe word with Mr. Jamieson if he can't take better care of you than this. Now good night, my dear. Sweet dreams."

She lifted her cheek for my salutation and smiled at me as I left the room.

The chocolate was very hot and strong, but I took a few sips of it while I cleansed my face, then I was so tired that I fell straight into bed, sleep claiming me at once. Physically, mentally and emotionally, the last few days had wrung me dry.

In my dreams there was nothing but bad omens. I was stalked by a black cat with burning green eyes and when it was about to leap on me its face became the face of the carving, the tongue a flame that licked at my skin, the horns white and sharp, and above me the invisible wings began to beat in quickening rhythm, growing louder and louder, their shadow filling all the skies. Closer and closer they came, engulfing me . . .

*   *   *

"Romaine!" a voice called from miles away. "Romaine, wake up!"

There were hands digging into me, shaking me. The wings faded and I came blurrily awake to stare at Peter's ravaged face.

"Thank God!" he breathed. "Sit up, Romaine. Sit!" He pulled at my shoulders, forcing me into a sitting position, and before I could comprehend what was happening he had hurried away, into the bathroom. The lamplight seemed intense and I covered my eyes with my hands as I heard Peter run water. A few moments later he was taking my hand, pressing a cold glass into it.

"Drink this. Are you awake yet? How do you feel?"

I sipped the water, still not understanding, trying to clear my head. A shiver ran through me as the air struck cold through my thin nightdress and the water reached my stomach, chilling it. Through a haze, I saw Peter's face again. He looked ill.

"Has something happened?" I asked.

Relief flooded through him. "You are awake! Do you still feel drowsy?"

"No, not really. Peter, whatever time is it? What is going on?" I gave him back the glass of water. "Will you pass my dressing gown, please? It's cold in here. There is something wrong, isn't there?"

He seemed determined not to answer my questions. Avoiding my eyes, he fetched my dressing gown, stopping to stare at the mug of chocolate which still stood on the corner of the vanity unit. With something between a sob and a laugh, he sat down on the ottoman at the foot of the bed, burying his head in his hands.

The last of the mist went away from my mind and I was fully awake. I reached for my watch, seeing that it was almost two o'clock. I had been in bed for only an hour and a half.

"You'd better tell me," I said, keeping my voice low because he was obviously distressed. "Is it grandmother?"

"Yes," the answer came hoarsely. "We've sent for the ambulance, but I'm afraid it will be too late. She collapsed . . . I thought you ought to know." Without looking at me, he tossed my dressing gown across the bed so that I could reach it; then he stood up, seeming distracted, and took the mug from the vanity unit, carrying it to the bathroom where he threw away the chocolate and rinsed out the mug, as if he had to be doing something.

Thrusting my arms into the quilted wrap, I slid my legs out of bed and felt for my slippers. "We must go down."

"There's nothing you can do," Peter said.

"Is your mother with her?"

"Yes."

He was right about our helplessness. We could only stand and watch grandmother's waxen face, listen to her laboured breathing. The ambulancemen were gentle as they lifted her onto a stretcher. Aunt Lydia went with them.

Roused by the commotion, Amy made coffee for Peter and me and we sat either side of the electric fire in the big drawing room, waiting for news.

" Were you with her when it happened?" I asked.

Peter looked across at me with bleary eyes. " What?"

" I said—were you with her? She was alone when I came in. I assumed everyone else was in bed, but . . . You're still dressed."

" Yes." He rubbed his face with both hands. " I came in late. She was waiting up for me. She does, sometimes. Oh, what does it matter?"

" I'm only trying to understand. What made her collapse?"

" Nothing! She's an old lady, that's all. It happens. She's had problems with her heart before, been taking drugs for it."

" If only she had left The Wood alone . . . "

" For God's sake!" He was on his feet, raging at me. " Can't you forget that idiotic superstition? If . . . " He stopped and we both looked towards the hall as the phone rang, then we glanced at each other uncertainly. After a moment, Peter went to answer the ringing.

I found myself in the doorway, listening as he spoke in monosyllables. Amy stood by the foot of the stairs, one hand to her mouth. Even though my cousin said very little it was clear from his voice that the news was not good. So my premonition had been right, but once again I had mistaken its victim. Grandmother had paid the price of defying the curse.

Very slowly, Peter put down the receiver and turned to look at Amy. " She's dead," he said quietly. " You'd better get back to bed. There's nothing else to do tonight. You, too, Romaine. I'm going to pick mother up."

*　　　*　　　*

I hardly slept, tormented by thoughts of Ricard Falconer and the evil he had wished on his descendants. There was, too, something else nagging at the back of my mind, something that refused to come forward, something which had not been entirely logical about that evening's happenings.

When dawn greyed the sky I decided to get up, dressed and went down to the kitchen to make myself a cup of coffee.

Almost without thinking about it, I had brought the empty mug which Peter had left in the bathroom, but it was not until I was placing it on the draining board that it awoke memories. Last night Peter had stopped dead when he saw the mug. He had emptied and rinsed it. All that after coming to wake me. I heard again the intense relief which had been in his voice when I had opened my eyes.

Suspiciously, I lifted the mug and sniffed at it, but no odour remained except the faintest hint of drinking chocolate. Maybe I was imagining things again. Grandmother herself had made the chocolate for me.

A sound behind made me whirl in alarm to see Peter watching me from the doorway. He looked terrible, pale and red-eyed, and he hadn't shaved.

"I didn't mean to startle you," he said, glancing at the mug I still had in my hand. "Are you making coffee? I couldn't sleep, either. I still can't believe it's happened."

"No," I said. "How's your mother?"

"Asleep. It was a shock to her, of course, so soon after Dad . . . But she'll be all right."

With my mind on other things, I made coffee and we sat at the big kitchen table to drink it, both of us tired and in no mood for conversation.

"What will you do now?" Peter asked at length.

"Do?"

"Well, you are her grand-daughter. If Jamieson . . . Did he mean what he said about wanting nothing from us?"

"I believe so. Must we talk about that now?"

"But it's important! As her heirs, we . . . "

I shook my head. "Not 'we', Peter. You. My father gave up his claim, didn't he? It will all be yours."

"Yes, but legally . . ." He seemed to be anxious about the

matter. "I happen to know that she made me her sole heir, but she did that months ago, before you ever came here. If there had been time she would have left it to us both."

It seemed odd that Peter should suddenly be so ready to share his inheritance with me. Perhaps my puzzlement showed on my face, for my cousin added:

"It's your right! Grandmother had a thing about not splitting the estate. That's one reason why ... Well, if you must know, she was against your father because she wanted to keep the estate intact, not split it between him and Dad. But I've never thought that was fair."

"I see," I said blankly. "But my father's dead, Peter. I've never expected, or wanted Falconsgarth. Let her have her final wish. I have no intention of contesting the Will."

He watched me in silence for a while, indecision written on his face. Finally he drew a deep breath and said, "I'll be honest with you, Romaine. The estate is badly in debt. And I mean badly. Grandmother's been trying to raise money— selling the hall, for one thing, and the oak from The Wood— but it would be a drop in the ocean. It's all my father's fault. He mismanaged everything. When I took over it was a mess and I've hardly been able to make any impression. The whole thing is going to pot. If we don't get some more capital from somewhere, Falconsgarth will have to be sold piecemeal."

"Then do that. There are things you could sell easily enough and raise thousands. The Rolls ... "

"The Rolls is part of the estate! Part of the tradition! She wouldn't let me touch it, or anything in the house. Besides, if I sell everything of value what will there be left to work for? I understand how she felt. I don't want to decimate the place, either."

"But you would have sold the hall," I said disgustedly, "which doesn't even belong to you. Or destroy The Wood, because it's something you can't understand. Well, grandmother's gone, Peter. You can do as you like now. Or are you still under her thumb?"

His lip curled, it may have been in self contempt. " It will

take some time to get used to the idea. I've never had a free
hand. She always knew what was best for Falconsgarth. And
the best thing would be money. Your mother was a rich
woman. You were her only daughter. She must have left
you . . ."

I stared at him in disbelief, not because of what he was saying but because of my own stupidity. Suddenly I understood
the meaning of what had been happening, and it all hinged
on the money to which I had barely given a thought. It was
true that my mother had been wealthy, but as yet the money
was tied up in property and legalities. I had not had time to
realise I was an heiress. Other things had seemed so much
more important. But grandmother hadn't forgotten, and
neither, it seemed, had Peter.

"Is that why she brought me here?" I breathed. "She
said she wanted to get to know me, but . . . Is that the reason?
Because of mother's money?"

He gazed unhappily at me. "Yes, I'm afraid so."

"But then . . ." It all fell into place—the reasons why
Peter had courted me so off-handedly, why he had gone to
the length of proposing marriage. Uncle Walter had tried to
warn me, hadn't he? 'You should never have come here,
Romaine.' Uncle Walter had suspected what they were up
to, his scheming mother and his son, but I, like a fool, had
been blind to their real intentions. It explained so much, in-
cluding their anger when I began seeing Tom. That had
upset their plans to pair me off with Peter.

And last night . . . again I glanced at the mug which had
held the chocolate prepared by grandmother's own hands;
the chocolate which Peter had made sure was poured away.
To destroy the evidence?

"She didn't mean it!" Peter burst out, as if he had read
my thoughts. "Those drugs she was taking sometimes made
her a bit woolly. Made her do things she would never have
done in her right mind."

"You mean she . . . she tried to kill me? If I had drunk
that chocolate. . . ."

" But you didn't, did you? Anyway, it might only have put you to sleep. I don't know. But I did try to prevent any harm, Romaine. I did come to wake you."

" She *told* you what she'd done?" I asked incredulously.

He shook his head as if he himself found it hard to believe. " She was desperate. We'd had a demand for repayment of a debt. And you were off with Jamieson all day . . . We all felt pretty sick about that. It was a betrayal, Romaine! Can't you see that? When I came in . . . she was angry with me. We had an argument and she let slip that she had put something in your drink. She said it would look as though you had done it yourself. Well, you *have* been behaving irrationally. But I told her she must be mad. She said I was as spineless as my father. Then she was in pain and fell . . . As soon as I fetched mother I came to wake you—to save you. She didn't really know what she was doing. She takes her tablets at night. They make her . . . odd."

Feeling sick, I stood up, glancing towards the door. I had to get away from here.

" Where are you going?" Peter demanded.

" To the cottage. I want to tell Tom what's happened. He's her grandson, too. He has a right to know."

I started across the kitchen, but somehow Peter was in front of me, barring the way. " It has nothing to do with him. You saw how he behaved the other day. It's between you and me, Romaine. We're the legitimate heirs. In partnership . . . "

" Do you think I would go into business with you?" I shouted. " Do you think I can't see what you've been doing? First it's marriage you offer, now a business arrangement. You've been as deeply involved in this as grandmother, doing everything she asked you . . . She was right! You *are* as weak as your father!"

His hand came up and I cowered away, realising that even now I could be in danger. If something happened to me, Peter was my nearest relative. He caught my wrist, his fingers grinding the bones together, his face working.

" Romaine! Romaine!" I was fighting him, my free hand

flailing until he caught that, too, pulling me close to him. "Romaine, listen to me!"

"If you don't let me go," I said through my teeth, "I shall scream. Amy will come, or your mother. Or are they in the plot, too?"

"There's no plot. Don't be stupid. We just hoped you would help. You have plenty of money and Falconsgarth has none. But you've turned your back. You prefer our enemies. How do you expect us to feel?"

"*Let me go!*"

He did so, stepping away from me, and I saw that his mouth was trembling. "What do you think I . . . Can you believe I'd harm you? Even now? I came to save you last night, for God's sake! If I had wanted you dead, I could have done it earlier. I could have put you off that cliff, you and Jamieson. I could have got rid of both of you, without anyone being the wiser. But I didn't. For a few minutes I was mad enough to think I could, but when it came to it . . . Not even grandmother could force me to become a murderer. Even though I was furiously angry. . . ."

I hung there, my head spinning. That car last night, on the coast road. "It was you?"

"Yes, it was me. She sent me after you. We *need* that money, Romaine! And you were with Jamieson—my half-brother. God!" His lips twisted. "If I'd been a killer I could have done it, easily. But I came to my senses. I knew then that nothing was worth the guilt I'd have to live with. Maybe I've gone along with grandmother so far. But that? No, I couldn't."

"Is that why she was angry with you?" I got out. "You hadn't done what she told you to do, so she was waiting to do it herself? Oh, Peter . . . " Bile rose in my throat and I pushed past him towards the door.

His voice followed me, saying flatly, "If you repeat any of this, I shall deny it. It's your word against mine. There's no proof. No proof at all."

It seemed to be miles through the mist to the cottage

where sanity and safety waited for me. I hammered on the door with the flat of my hand, shaking and calling for Tom, and suddenly he was there. I flung myself into his arms, holding him tightly, realising slowly that he was wet, wrapped only in a towel. His skin was smooth and smelt warmly of soap and my hands slid across his back, caressing him in an agony of gratitude that he was there.

"Romaine . . . " He forced me a little away from him, looking down at me in concern. " Darling, what . . . "

" Grandmother," I managed. " She died last night. Her heart . . . Oh, Tom, they tried to kill me! I can't go back there. Please let me stay with you."

He drew me to him again, his mouth hard on mine, his hands moving across my shoulders, my spine, his body pressed against me. For a few moments there was nothing else in all the world but our need of each other; then it must have registered with him what I had said, for he tore his mouth away and looked at me with burning eyes.

"What did you say? They tried . . . My God, I'll . . . "

" Tom," Ruth's voice said gently from behind him. " Don't you think you ought to get dressed?"

Tom wanted action. He would have called the police, except that Peter had been right when he said there was no proof. Then he wanted to go to Falconsgarth and have it out with Peter, which would have meant violence. Tom was in no mood for polite conversation. Between us, Ruth and Connan and I persuaded him that fighting with Peter would solve nothing and eventually he calmed down enough to eat the breakfast his mother had prepared.

We all sat in the kitchen, discussing what had occurred.

" Peter let himself be used," was Ruth's opinion. " Lady Faulkner was good at using people. Her husband, her sons . . . She was a wicked old woman. May God forgive her."

Tom had been silent for some time and it seemed that he had been thinking over the story which I had told so incoherently.

" What I don't understand," he said, " is why they were so

anxious to embroil you in it. Did she want to marry you off
to Peter to prevent the estate being split?"

"That may have been part of it," I said wearily, not liking
what I had to do now. "But the real reason . . . Didn't I say
why? I hoped you would have realised. I thought uncle Walter
might have told you."

"Told me what?"

"That I'm going to be a rich woman. Mother left everything she had to me."

He watched me, uncomprehending. "I don't follow. Your
mother?"

"Don't you know who she was? Tom, my mother was
Merielle Dupris. I'm not very proud of the fact, considering
the reputation she gained for herself these last few years, but
it's true."

He blinked slowly three times, as if to wake himself up.
"Merielle Dupris? The actress? But . . . Do you mean that
you were with her when she was killed? It said in the papers
. . ."

"It said the passenger was her secretary, I know. That's
another story. Until that last few weeks I had hardly seen her
since my father died. I was a translator for a publishing firm.
I have a tiny flat. I was just like millions of other girls. I do
vaguely remember signing papers when I was in hospital, to
let the lawyers deal with everything, but it hasn't been real
to me until recently. If I had realised sooner . . . But grandmother seemed so fragile. I never dreamed she was capable of
. . ." The words trailed off as I saw the way he was looking
at me. "Does it make any difference?"

"I shall have to give it some thought," he said doubtfully.
"Damn it, I assumed you were the poor relation. If I had
known from the start I'd never have dared . . ."

"Does it make any difference?" I asked again.

His eyes held mine, in them a speculation that slowly
warmed into love. "To the way I feel?" he said eventually.
"No, nothing can change that."

Our hands met and clasped tightly, then Connan cleared

his throat as if to remind us that he and Ruth were still there.

"What shall you do now, Romaine?" he asked. "Will you go back to Falconsgarth?"

"She will not!" Tom said firmly. "She can have my room. I can sleep on the settee for a while. She's not going back to that place except just long enough to pack her things. And *I'm* going with her."

"And The Wood?" Connan said.

"We must wait and see what Evan says," I told him.

*   *   *

At Falconsgarth we were met with tight-lipped silence from Peter. When I told him I intended to collect my things and move into the cottage temporarily he shrugged and walked away. His mother was coming down the stairs, but she felt differently.

"Have you no respect?" she hissed with a glance at Tom. "To bring *him* here. . . ."

"He won't be here for long," I replied. "And neither shall I. Excuse me."

It was strange, but Falconsgarth itself no longer held any menace for me. I have often wondered if the malevolence I sensed at the house was grandmother's and nothing to do with Ricard Falconer, the witch.

*   *   *

At The Wood, however, the feeling of evil remained. It was a subdued little party which gathered there in the mist of a late November morning: Connan, Tom and myself, and Evan, whose bishop had agreed that he should perform the ceremony. Peter had also given his grudging permission, though Evan told us he had muttered darkly about pagan rites and idiotic females. But although he scoffed he seemed to think it might be safer if the curse was laid.

We gathered round Ricard Falconer's tomb, where the air

was alive, making the hairs on my nape stand up, prickling. The words were said and the holy water sprinkled, and suddenly there was a stillness. The sun came out briefly and a lone bird began to twitter. Both Connan and I felt it. Ricard Falconer was at rest at last.

As we left the place, we encountered Peter, who must have been waiting to see what would happen.

"Are you satisfied now?" he demanded. "I'm surprised at you all, especially you, Evan. You're supposed to be a Christian, yet . . ." The words were bitten off. He must have realised he was blustering. He shrugged his shoulders, hunched deeper into his coat. "I'd like a word with you, Romaine, if you don't mind."

Evan and Connan took the hint and began to move away towards the cottage, where Ruth had said she would have a pot of coffee waiting for us. With a bleak glance at Tom, Peter took my arm and edged me a few feet away.

"You haven't reconsidered, have you?"

"No, Peter. I'm sorry, but what money I have I shall need. We're going to buy a farm—and there's the hall."

"The hall?"

"Haven't you had another offer for it? . . . Yes, I thought so. I arranged it with my lawyers. I'm buying the place. I shall give it back to the W.I., where it rightfully belongs, though they needn't know. If you like, you can present them with the deed yourself and put right the wrong that has been done. That far, I'm prepared to help. The money should give you a small breathing space."

He thrust his hands into his coat pockets, looking down at his shoe toes before lifting his eyes to my face. "Why? Why would you do that?"

"Because I think my father would have wished it. Because it's time the village stopped hating the Faulkners. They call us 'the Devil's breed', you know. But we aren't all bad."

"No," Peter said dully. "Only weak and spineless . . . except, it seems, for our women folk."

"Will you have The Wood felled now?" I asked.

He glanced at the silent trees looming through the mist behind us. " No, I think not. Let it stand. Not that it frightens me," he added hastily, " but ... There's such a thing as tempting fate. All the same, Romaine, your famous curse will probably come true."

" How do you mean?"

" Well, if you remember, it doesn't say that the Faulkners will die out, does it? Not in the version I was brought up with, anyway. It says, ' If The Wood falls, the Faulkners will disappear from the valley '. And if I have to sell up and move I shall go far away. It might be the best course. There's nothing here except bad memories. And as for you ... Even if you stay in the district you won't be a Faulkner any more. I assume you and Tom ... "

" Yes."

" So there you are. Ricard Falconer has the last laugh. Goodbye, Romaine."

He held out his hand and after a brief hesitation I took it. There had been feuds enough.

" Goodbye, Peter."

Together, Tom and I watched him go, poor Peter who had inherited very little. The Faulkners had finally come to the end of their long reign in this corner of Exmoor. Then we turned our backs on Falconer's Wood and walked hand in hand down the hill, where the puppy Gypsy came bounding to greet us.